Series

Prairie Dawn's

Native Warrior

5th Book

Karen Dee Musson

Disclaimer

This book is a work of fiction intended for entertainment purposes only.
Any resemblance to real people, events, places, or organizations is
purely coincidental. The characters and scenarios are products of the
author's imagination. While inspired by cultural or historical references,
the content should not be taken as fact.

Dedication

This book is dedicated to Kimberly Vergonet, Elizabeth, Medicine Moon, Martinez, and my Lord Jesus Christ.

A very special thank you to Millie Van Gundy, Millie Musson and my sister Konnie for all your dedication and time. This book would not be possible without you.

List of Characters

White Horse | Chief of Lakota band, and husband to Prairie Dawn.

Prairie Dawn | Carrie's Indian name and wife to White Horse.

Koawa | Lakota warrior and brother to White Horse.

Blue Thunder | Lakota warrior and like a brother to Prairie Dawn.

Grey Wolf | Lakota warrior.

Eagle Moon | Young Lakota warrior.

Kikimo | Youth and son to White Horse from his deceased wife, before he met Prairie Dawn.

Little Foot | Child and son to White Horse and Prairie Dawn.

Morning Dove | Child, Koawa's daughter.

Medicine Moon | Cheyenne medicine woman.

Night Eagle | Medicine Moon when she becomes a warrior.

Minoke | Lakota woman and aunt to Kikimo.

Song Bird | Lakota woman.

Rising Sun | Youth, White Horse's illegitimate daughter.

Roger | Carrie's brother and known to the Lakota as Great Healer.

Rose | Roger's wife.

Max | Roger's dog.

Little Fox | Matthew's Indian name and Blue Thunder's son.

Stella | Matthew's mother and Blue Thunder's love interest.

General Phillips | General of the Fort.

Rose Petal | Stella's Indian name.

Spirit Dog | Kikimo's beloved horse.

Prologue

A blanket of wildflowers and tall grass cross the Great Plains, as White Horse sits high on a hill overlooking his band, as they move to a new home thanks to his brother-in-law Roger tipping him off, he was able to move his camp early this morning before the Blue Coat's attacked. They will reach their new camp by sundown.

General Phillips is fuming as he looks at the abandoned Lakota camp. He is certain by the still smoldering campfires that he has not missed them by more than a few hours. He is growing incredibly frustrated and tired on this allusive band of Lakota's always staying one step ahead of him. He cannot understand how they are doing it. One of his soldiers rides up beside him.

"Sir, we picked up their tracks just East of here. Would you like for us to follow them sir?"

"No soldier," he growls.

"You sure sir? They have not been gone long."

"Soldier, have you ever heard of a coy dog?"

"No sir I have not."

"I learned what one was when I was stationed in Arizona to bring in some Apache's. A coy dog is a dog that has a reputation of stealing and avoiding detection."

"I am not following you sir."

"Those tracks are from a coy dog soldier, meaning they will lead us into circles."

"I see sir. What is the orders sir," the soldier asks?

"We head back to the Fort and regroup."

"Yes sir."

Chapter One

Rose Petal

A breeze gently flows through Blue Thunder's hair, as he is sitting high on his horse gazing down at the Orphanage below. He is a man who fears nothing, but at this moment his heart is racing with anxiety, with the anticipation of meeting the son, he just recently found out he has. He remembers back a few months ago, being told by his Chief of a child that was conceived by the White Woman who he had a short relationship with in Willow Creek, nearly eight years ago. Her name was Stella, or Rose Petal as he called her. She is also Prairie Dawn's best friend. He met his Rose Petal when he was in Willow Creek helping his Chief in retaliating against a band of renegade Indians, who were terrorizing the small town. He would sit with her under the great apple tree as she mourned the loss of her parents that were killed in one of the many attacks. He remembers consoling her and allowing her to cry in his arms. Their romance quickly blossomed and soon became intimate. He remembers how devastated he was when his Rose Petal refused to join him when it came time to return home. If he had known that she was with child at that time, he never would have allowed her to stay.

He gazes over at his Chief sitting on his horse beside him. His heart grows soft, as he reflects at how much he idolizes this man. Blue Thunder remembers the day when White Horse became Chief.

It was the same day that his dear friend lost both his father, who was Chief, and his first wife, Flowering Blossom in a Pawnee attack. He remembers how grief stricken his Chief was. He has known this man for his entire life and remembers the many times they would play and hunt together when they were boys. Although only a few years separate them in age, he considers White Horse as a father and would die to protect him. He looks across from his Chief to the man beside him, Koawa, the Chief's younger brother. He loves this man like he was kin and they virtually go everywhere together. He knows Koawa like the back of his hand and there is nothing that he wouldn't do for him.

He then turns his head the other direction and grins to himself when he sees the young warrior who he helped train, Grey Wolf. He is proud of what a strong warrior that this man has become and is honored to fight alongside of him when they are in a battle. He then turns his attention over to the newest member in the band, Night Eagle. She is as beautiful as a sunset, but has the strength of a warrior. In just the few months she has been in the band, she has captured the heart of Grey Wolf and has become Prairie Dawn's best friend. Her wisdom and ability to carry her own is what gave her the warrior's name of Night Eagle, but she goes by Medicine Moon, her birth name, when she is healing.

His attention is drawn away to the woman with the golden hair who is riding alongside of him, the Chief's wife, Prairie Dawn. After many years of trying and several miscarriages, the spirits have finally blessed her and his Chief with another child and she is roughly six months along. He considers this woman as a sister and over the years has grown to admire her strength and courage. They have been through a great deal together and he would crush any man who tried to hurt her. He catches her smiling over at him.

"Are you ready to meet your son?" she asks him in his tongue.

"Yes," he answers. "I am ready."

"You have spent many months preparing yourself for this

day" White Horse tells him. "Are you sure you want all of us here when you meet your son for the first time?"

"Yes, I will need Prairie Dawn to translate for me and I will need all of you here in the event I am not welcomed and she has sent the Army in to capture me."

"Great Healer will see to it that you are treated well," White Horse says. "But if you are certain that we will not be in your way, then we are honored to join you."

"It is I who is honored. Thank you, my Chief for allowing your wife in her condition to join us."

"I believe I can speak for my wife, when I say that there is nothing that would keep her away from such a day as this."

With that said, we begin our descent down the hill and start the short walk to the Orphanage.

Roger stands on the grand porch and waits patiently alongside his dog Max, for his guests to make the rest of their journey down the hill. He saw them standing on the hill when he looked out from the big bay window from the room that he uses as his personal quarters when he is at the Orphanage. He knew that they were close when he saw White Horse's scouts a few days ago when he was in the garden with his wife. He knows that is a sign that his brother-in-law and sister were only a few days away. He glances over at his wife Rose, when he hears her step outside.

"She is as nervous as a child who just got caught with their hand in a cookie jar." she tells him.

"I imagine that Blue Thunder is just as nervous, if not more," he tells her.

"I am so excited to see Carrie! I cannot wait to tell her that she will be an aunt in only a few short months."

"She will be just as excited as I am," he tells her, before kissing her hand. Their tender moment ends when they see their guest approaching. Max is the first to bolt away and rush off to greet them.

3

"Welcome," Roger says to White Horse, as his guests bring their horses to a stop. Roger watches, as one by one they dismount. He walks over to his sister to help her off. When she jumps down, he quickly sees that she too is with child. He brings her into his arms and tightly embraces her.

"I have missed you my sister," he says.

"As have I," I tell him. He brings me out of his embrace and gazes down at me. "You just get more beautiful every time I see you," he tells me.

"Oh Roger," I blush. He looks down at the small bulge that signals to everyone that I am with child.

"I am so happy for you," he tells me.

"Thank you, Roger. We are both delighted that our spirits have blessed us again."

White Horse joins me by my side. Roger greets him with a handshake. "You are looking good Chief," Roger tells him.

"I see congratulations are in order for your upcoming arrival."

"Thank you," White Horse grins. A quick welcome is made by Roger to our other guest, as White Horse takes a few moments to greet Max. Roger then looks over at Blue Thunder.

"Stella and the boy are inside," he tells him. White Horse translates.

Upon stepping on the porch, I am quickly greeted by Rose. It is then that we all see that she too is expecting. I am thrilled by the news and am quickly giving her a hug. Our visit is cut short by White Horse who is gently nudging me to go inside.

"We will have time to visit later," he tells me. "We must attend first to the reason we came."

"Certainly dear," I tell him.

It has been many months since I have seen either Roger or Rose and I want to stay and visit, but my husband is correct and now is not the time to think of me. I smile up at him.

"We will wait for you by the creek," he tells me, before I head inside.

We follow Roger inside. My mouth nearly drops in amazement from the richness of the house.

"The Orphanage was once the home to a very wealthy Army Captain," Roger begins to explain. "Despite his wealth, he had a very hard life. His wife died of consumption and his only child died in a tragic accident at a young age. He took care of his mother when her health failed up to the day she died. He was a man who kept to himself and had little friends, but by what I remember of our father telling me, he had a heart of gold. He routinely donated his money to Father's Orphanage. When he died Father was willed this home. He never had any use for it and would rent it out to anyone who was willing to pay the hefty price. When our father died, this home was part of my inheritance. When the orphanage in Cedar Brook became so run down, I opened this up and made it into the Orphanage."

The place is huge and there is plenty of space for rambunctious children to run around in. There is a grand staircase that flows through the room and a ceiling that nearly touches the sky. Blue Thunder and I are both in awe with the magnitude of the home.

"Why would anyone want to be closed in by a box instead of being free with nature is beyond me," Blue Thunder mumbles. I couldn't help but chuckle at his comment.

"I have ordered that the children remain in their classroom with the sisters until you all have left. They are all upstairs. You should not have any problems," Roger says.

"And where is Stella and Matthew?" I ask him.

"He and Stella are in the sitting room. I will show you the way."

Stella is sitting on the lounger next to her seven-year-old son. Her insides are filled with anxiety with anticipation of seeing Blue Thunder after all these years. She finally told Matthew the truth on who his real father is and believes that he understands it. She is concerned about Blue Thunder and how he is going to react when he sees his son for the first time. Roger had assured her that everything would be alright and Blue Thunder was not upset with her and was anxious to see her and Matthew. But she cannot help but wonder if this is true, as she would not put it past Roger to just tell her that so she would leave that filthy railroad town to come here.

She remembers Blue Thunder as being a very calm and loving man towards her and she remembers how much she loved him. It pained her to leave him behind, but she was too scared to leave the comfortable life she had with Hank to follow him. Her thoughts are interrupted when she hears Roger's boots on the floor outside of the room. Stella takes a deep breath and exhales when she hears the click of the doorknob being turned. She quickly straightens out her dress and touches up her hair before the door opens. Matthew rises to his feet when he hears the doorknob turn. He is quickly stopped when his mother takes his hand and motions for him to sit back down. The door is then opened and Roger is the first to be seen stepping in.

We are taken into a smaller room that is darker and less inviting. It is rich in appearance with the mahogany wood that is seen throughout it, but despite its rich appearance the room is dreary and plain.

"This used to be the Captain's mother's room," Roger says. "The Captain never changed anything after she died and this part of the house is rarely used."

That explains a lot, I think to myself. There is stillness in the air when eye contact is met with Stella. Despite the slight ageing on her face, she has not changed a bit.

"Stella," I smile. I quickly rush to give her a hug when she rises to her feet. She is a little timid to hug me back and makes it very subtle and quick, as she spots Blue Thunder from over my shoulder.

You could hear a pin drop in the room from the tension that she was suffering looking up at him. I see Blue Thunder grin at her. This seemed to lighten her up and she was more relaxed that we were here. Roger motions for a little boy, who I am assuming is Matthew, to come to him then Blue Thunder takes his hand into his. The little boy looks up at the Indian in front of him. I am certain, by the awe on his face that this is the first time that he has ever seen an Indian up close. Blue Thunder is a magnificent warrior and he carries himself with great pride and dignity. He is soft spoken and extremely mellow, unless provoked and then he is the wickedest person to be around with a worse temper than White Horse.

"Blue Thunder, this is Matthew, your son," Roger tells him.

Matthew has fair skin with jet black hair and the biggest darkest eyes that shine like marbles. Although he carries a lot of his mother's traits, there is no mistaken that he has his father's eyes. There is no need for me to translate, no introductions are needed as Blue Thunder knows exactly who he is. I watch him come down on one knee. He removes a necklace from around his neck and places it over Matthew's. Matthew looks down at the necklace around his neck and then up at Blue Thunder. He then rushes into his father's embrace. It was such a tender moment that I nearly cried.

Roger takes it upon himself and excuses himself to join White Horse and the others by the creek so Blue Thunder can be alone to talk with Stella. He takes Matthew with him so both sides are free to talk in private. Because of the language barrier, Blue Thunder asks that I remain so I can translate. We all find our separate places and sit down. Blue Thunder is the first to break the ice.

"You look beautiful Rose Petal," he grins. I translate.

"Thank you," she says shyly.

"Our son, he looks strong."

"Yes, he is," she says. "He loves to go outside. He plays too much." He grins over at her.

"In the many years that we have been apart, I have never stopped thinking of you. The woman who smelled like a flower and is as radiant as the sun." As I translate it to her, she blushes. Blue Thunder continues.

"I have had many months to prepare my mind on having a son. I would stay awake many nights wondering how he was doing and how his mother was."

"Blue Thunder," Stella begins. "I am so sorry. You should have been told sooner, but I was too scared. I was afraid for Matthew and what you would do to him if you found out. I was afraid that you might take him away because you were angry with me for not telling you about him."

Blue Thunder grew still a moment after I translated to him. He then reaches across the chair and takes Stella's hand into his.

"I can understand why you would think that, but never would I hurt you or our son. You are my Rose Petal."

It took everything I had to keep my composer to translate to Stella the deep sentimental words that were spoken by this mighty and magnificent strong warrior. I have known Blue Thunder for many years and consider this man as a brother. I know a great deal about him and his behavior and never have I ever heard him open up this much or go this far deep into his emotions with anyone. To witness this shows me how much he really loves her, even after all these years. After I translated this to her, I put my two cents in.

"I know this man almost as well as my husband and he has never spoken this deep before to anyone. He is sincere Stella. He loves you and his son."

Stella starts to wipe a tear that is rolling down her cheek. Blue Thunder intervenes, by catching the tear drop with his thumb. She then speaks.

"I want what is best for Matthew. It has been so hard on him. Children can be so cruel. He has never had many friends. I want to give him a better life, but his life is so different than ours. I don't think I can survive it. I am not strong like you Carrie."

"It is hard at times. I will admit it, but you learn to survive. It is a good life. They are amazing people. I would never go back to my previous life. I love them too much and I love White Horse too much to even consider it." Blue Thunder is wondering what is being said and why his Rose Petal is so upset. I take a few moments and translate. He reaches up and strokes her hair.

"You and I live in different worlds, but our hearts are as one. I have not come to take you away. As much as I want this, I know that it would be too hard on you and our son as you are not used to our ways. We have lost many during these harsh times and I fear for both of your safety. There are many times when I will not return home for several days. During these times, you would be alone. Prairie Dawn would take care of you when I am unable too, but I fear that you would not be happy. I feel that you need to be here at least for now. I will come to visit when I can. I will have Prairie Dawn ask Great Healer if he can bring you closer, that way I can see you and our son more often."

I will admit that I am a little shocked, as I would have bet money that Blue Thunder would fight to bring her along. This just goes to show me how much love he has for this woman and his child and just how unselfish he really is. I translate to Stella what he says. She seemed just as surprised as me and relieved.

"Roger mentioned to me that there is an opening in the Fort for a seamstress," she says. "I am certain that when I tell Roger what is going on he will help me," she says.

"I am sure he will," I tell her. I translate one final time to Blue Thunder. He nods his head and smiles over at Stella. He glances up at me and motions for me to leave. I do as he wishes and excuse myself and leave to find my husband.

Chapter Two

The Reunion

Roger and Matthew make their way to the creek to join the others. Roger spots his wife standing next to White Horse conversing. When they see him, they stop their conversation and smile over at him. Roger is well known throughout the band as their Great Healer and his presence is warmly accepted by the other warriors. As he passes by them on his way to White Horse and his wife, he is greeted with pats on the back and handshakes. Upon seeing all the warriors around him, Matthew cowards into Roger's side.

"Relax my child," Roger says. "These men are peaceful and you will treat them with respect."

"Who are they?" the boy asks.

"They are Lakota, just like your father is," Roger answers.

They continue their way through until they are greeted by White Horse. He looks down at Matthew. He notices that he is very similar in color to his own son, Little Foot, and that the half-breed is very apparent in him. Despite this though, the Lakota is strongly seen in his facial features and in his dark, shiny, thick hair. He can see the fear in the boy's eyes and he is certain that this is the first time he has ever seen so many of his kind up close. White Horse looks down at Matthew.

"I am Chief White Horse," he tells Matthew. "Do not fear me, for we are friends."

"Are you a real Indian?" he asks him.

"Matthew!" Roger scolds.

"It is alright," White Horse says. "It is only natural for a boy his age to be curious." He looks down at Matthew.

"Yes Matthew, I am."

"Do you know my father?" Matthew asks him.

"Yes," he answers. "I know him very well."

"How come you speak English, but my father doesn't?"

White Horse comes down to eye level to the boy.

"When I was about your age my father, who was Chief at the time, saved a White Man from a raging river. He brought this man to my lodge. He stayed many months with us. My father wanted my brother and myself to learn the White Man tongue in the event we ever needed to use it in trading. This man taught us, for many months I would only speak his tongue. While other boys like your father were playing games, I was inside my lodge studying. That is why I know your language and not your father."

"Maybe you can teach me yours," Matthew says.

"Maybe," White Horse grins.

"Matthew," Rose interrupts, "Why don't we find some flowers to pick in the meadow for your mother."

"Awe," Matthew whines, "Do we have to?"

"Matthew," Roger says. "Do not give any argument. You do as you are told. You have asked the Chief enough questions for one day."

"Oh, alright," he huffs.

"You watch your step dear," Roger says to his wife. "I do not want you tripping and taking a spill."

"Oh Roger," she barks. "Honestly, sometimes you say the most foolish things." "It is not foolish dear. Women in an advanced stage of pregnancy are prone to be clumsy. It is not something that you can help."

Rose adores her husband and cannot remember seeing him so happy as he was the day that she told him that she was late for her monthly by two months. He was hardly able to control himself with excitement after he confirmed her pregnancy. He has pampered her more than usual during this time and seldom does he allow her to do much on her own, even though she reminds him that he tells other expectant patients differently. She leans up and kisses his cheek. "I will be careful dear, I promise."

He watches his wife and Matthew walk the short distance to the meadow, before turning his attention back to White Horse.

"I do apologize White Horse," Roger says.

"Do not worry for this. My wife is the same with me," he smiles. "By the looks of Rose and my Prairie Dawn, our off springs will only be born a few months apart."

"Yes," Roger agrees. "I will make sure that there are plenty of roots for Carrie when she delivers."

"Yes, we will stay close until her time, so it will be picked fresh."

"How have things been White Horse?" Roger asks him.

"We are doing alright. My gratitude to you as we barely escaped that attack a few weeks back."

"I am glad I overheard the General's plan on it," Roger says.

"We are safe now," White Horse says. "Hidden in the hollow of the hills we should be able to stay there until after the birth.'

"General Phillips still believes that you are dead. I believe that is helping you, at least for the time being," Roger says.

"You may be correct however, I believe he is no fool and he knows that someone is taking my place. It is just a matter of time before we meet again."

"I wish I could do more to help you."

"You are brother. By keeping an eye on where he and his men are, is keeping me one step ahead of him."

"If Rose knew I was doing this…" White Horse puts his hand up to silence Roger.

"Say no more," he says. "I have already received the lecture from my wife. I do not want you to do anything that you feel uncomfortable about. The last thing I want is any harm to come to you because of me."

"White Horse, I am doing this because I want to. I refuse to sit back and watch the people that I love be annihilated."

"You are a good man, Roger." White Horse smiles.

Upon stepping off the porch, I immediately see my husband and brother standing underneath a tree. I make my way over to them. Roger takes my hand.

"My sister you look radiant," he says hugging her.

"Thank you," I smile. "I feel like a balloon ready to pop."

"It is awfully warm out and you have been traveling, are you staying hydrated?" Roger asks.

"White Horse sees to it and before you ask, I am resting as well." Roger faintly grins.

"How did you know I was going to ask you that?"

"I know my brother," I tease. White Horse interrupts the conversation by putting his arm around my expanding waist.

"I understand your desire on wanting to visit with your brother my Prairie Dawn, but we really must be moving on."

"I understand," I tell him. "I know Blue Thunder has much to discuss with you as well."

"I can see the joy on his face, we were correct in bringing him here."

White Horse has his warriors gathered and everyone has said their goodbyes. Blue Thunder comes down on one knee in front of Matthew. He shows his son the necklace that he is wearing around his neck and then points to Matthew.

"His is just like yours," White Horse translates. "You both wear yours and you will never be far apart."

The tender moment almost brought tears to Stella's eyes. I watch Blue Thunder come to a stand and jump on his horse. He briefly stares down at Stella and gives her a sweet grin. He then turns his horse around and joins the others.

Roger reaches up and squeezes my hand. "You rest often and keep your feet propped up so they don't swell. Have White Horse bring you to my place a week after you return home, so I can properly monitor you and the baby."

Although Medicine Moon was taking excellent care of me, I give my brother no argument and agree to return to him shortly.

Roger places his arm around his wife, as they watch the Lakota's ride off into the horizon.

Little George and Timmy are looking out the upstairs classroom window at all the Lakota warriors near the water.

"Wow have you seen so many?" Timmy says.

"I think there Cheyenne or maybe Pawnee," George says.

"Nah, there are Sioux," Timmy argues.

"How would you know?"

"When General Phillips takes me fishing, he talks about them damn Sioux."

"You are so lucky that General Phillips and the Mrs. will be your new Ma and Pa."

"Yes, as soon as the paperwork is finished, I will have a new home." Suddenly George points to the window.

"Look, there's Doctor Briggs with that half breed."

"Them damn Sioux sure seem to like Doctor Briggs. Look how they are patting him on the back. I wonder who that blonde woman is who is hugging the doctor?" Timmy wonders.

They watch as Roger converses with White Horse.

"That one looks of importance, like a Chief or something."

"Boy, wait until I tell the General that I saw the damn Sioux." Timmy says.

"Boys!" they hear. They rush back to their chairs and sit down when Sister Ann comes in front of them.

"Why are you not studying your sums like I instructed?"

"Timmy just wanted to see the Indians," George squeals.

"Never mind that. You two know better than to be out of your chairs."

"It was just for a second," Timmy argues.

"I want you both to write down ten bible verses and have them memorized by tomorrow."

"Aww, do we have to," George whines.

"Yes, you do and if you keep arguing I will make it twenty."

Chapter Three
The Mother's

Four days later and further down the Prairie, Eagle Moon stands proud in his lodge that he shares with his adopted mother, Medicine Moon. He was recently orphaned in the last attack that nearly wiped out the Lakota camp. Although he is nearly seventeen years in age and can take care of himself, he is grateful that Medicine Moon stepped in and opened her heart to him during the most difficult time in his life. She took him under her wing and immediately became a mother figure to him and along with Grey Wolf, has taught him to become a fine warrior. He admires Medicine Moon not only for her wisdom in healing, but for her strength and knowledge that she has taught him. When he had his naming ceremony it only seemed fit that he received the name of Eagle Moon, a combination of Medicine Moon the healer and Night Eagle the Warrior Princess. He stands up patiently and waits for his mother to finish the last touches to his war tunic.

"I should not keep Grey Wolf waiting," he tells her.

"It is not Grey Wolf who is growing impatient," she says. "It is you."

"It looks good," he whines. "Any White Man would fear me in this."

Your arrogance will get you killed," Medicine Moon scolds.

"That is not what Grey Wolf told me and he is a great warrior," he argues.

"He is great because he uses his mind and is patient, which is more than I can say for you."

He smirks down at her and says, "I am what I am today because of you both. You both works well together." She glances up at him.

"What is that supposed to mean?" she says. "I do not understand why you are fighting it. You lost your family too and you grieved heavy. Your heart will always miss them. Grey Wolf is a wonderful man, a magnificent warrior and a skilled hunter. He would do well for you. He could fill that void that you are missing."

He can tell by the look that she is giving him that she is embarrassed. It has never been a secret to anyone who sees them together that they are both smitten with each other. He even caught them by accident kissing in the woods and he is certain that it was not the first time that they had exchanged a kiss. She steps back to examine her work and straighten out a crease.

"You are ready to go," she says.

"You are ignoring me," he grins.

"Stay focused," she snaps. "The Pawnee are not easy to fool. They are bitter enemies of the Lakota and will have no mercy on any of you. You listen to Grey Wolf and you do everything that he tells you to do, and never lose your focus."

"You and Grey Wolf have taught me well. I will be fine," he boasts. "The arrows that I have made will soar high with the added touch of an eagle feather that I have put on them. The one who falls from it will know that it was me, Eagle Moon, proud and strong warrior."

"Your arrows may pierce the enemy's heart, and show that you are a strong warrior, but it will do nothing for you if you are inpatient."

Eagle Moon just rolled his eyes. Before any more can be said, Grey Wolf steps into the lodge.

"We will be leaving soon," he says. "Go prepare yourself and your war pony for battle." Eagle Moon does as he is told and leaves the lodge. Grey Wolf smiles over to Medicine Moon. He takes her hand into his.

"Do not worry your pretty mind," he tells her. "He is ready."

"It is not him that I am concerned about, it is you," she says.

"I am more than capable of taking on any Pawnee," he tells her.

"I wish you would allow me to go. I know what he looks like and I know his habits. Night Eagle would fight well alongside of you."

"Grey Wolf has no doubt that you are able to slice a Pawnee warrior's throat. We have been over this already. I must go alone with the other warriors. The Chief trusts me to lead the others into battle, instead of Koawa or Blue Thunder. I will bring you the scalp of the one who defiled you and killed your family. You will get your revenge Medicine Moon, I promise you."

"I want to see you slice his throat and watch his eyes as he looks at the fear of death in front of him."

Grey Wolf gently strokes Medicine Moon's cheek. "I need to do this alone," he tells her. He can see the disappointment in her eyes.

"Prairie Dawn is with child and may need you when I am gone. The Chief is depending on you to be here for her, because Great Healer is so far away."

"You make a good argument and as always are wise with your words. I wish you well on your journey my Grey Wolf," she says.

I come up alongside of Medicine Moon, who is standing near the corral of horses watching Grey Wolf and his selected group of young warriors mount up. I watch him faintly grin over at her, before turning his pony around and riding off with the others.

"They will be alright," I tell her. She smiles over at me, before walking back towards her lodge.

Several days later, Roger is patiently sitting at the table waiting for Rose to serve his dinner. He is feeling relaxed this evening and looking forward to a quiet evening with his wife. Since the arrival of Stella and Matthew from the Orphanage, his life and home has been turned upside down and he has had to make several adjustments to his everyday life to accommodate them.

Roger convinced General Phillips wife to hire Stella on a day-to-day trial basis as her personal seamstress and chamber maid. Stella has been putting in a lot of hours and she seems to be doing very well. He is praying that the position will turn into full time by the end of the month. He made the loft up for Stella and Matthew to stay in. Although they are unable to stand upright in it and are a little cramped, he has heard no complaints from her and they seemed to be comfortable. The old chest that blocks the entrance to the cavern remains in place and Stella has never questioned as to why it is there. Due to the lack of storage Roger agreed to allow Stella to use it to store her and Matthew's belongings in.

He looks across at his wife as his plate is placed in front of him and she sits down. He smiles at her, as she places her napkin on her lap.

"What," she asks, grinning over at him.

"You look radiant," he smiles.

"I look like a heifer," she says.

"The most beautiful heifer I have ever seen," he grins.

"Shut up Roger," she smiles, as she adjusts her napkin on her lap. Roger takes no offense to his wife's comment and chuckles.

"Sure, is quiet around here this evening" he says on a lighter note.

"Yes, it is nice for a change. I truly do enjoy having Stella and Matthew around here, but I miss just us," she says.

"Me too, that is why I offered Stella to take the wagon for the evening and go into the Fort and have dinner with the General and his wife. It is good for both to mingle with the other society of life."

"I have had several tea parties with his wife," Rose says, "and I am a little surprised that she finds Stella's standards high enough to share her dinner table with."

"Well, I must confess that I had something to do with that," Roger grins.

"What did you do?" Rose smiled.

"I just asked him for a favor, He has filled out paperwork to adopt Timmy at the Orphanage. I think he wants to have Matthew there so his wife will get used to having a child around that is roughly the same age."

"Humph!" she says.

"I did it for you my Love," he says, as he reaches across the table to squeeze her hand. "So, we can have a peaceful dinner together. Once the baby arrives, we will not have much of an opportunity to be alone."

He watches her face go sad and she quickly takes her hand out of his. Roger knows his Rose very well and understands what great pride she takes in her appearance. She is looking very tired and worn out and is at the stage of her pregnancy where her face is full and her body is retaining water weight. She is only a few weeks away from giving birth and knows that the last trimester is the hardest and longest time for a woman. He has seen it time and time again in other women patients that he has cared for during their pregnancy and understands how many of them feel less attractive. He does not want this to happen to his wife, so he comes up with an idea to help boost her spirits.

"Darling, I have an idea," he says. "Our child is due for arrival in a few weeks and we barely have anything for it. Tomorrow, I have to be at the Fort early in the morning, but the rest of the day I do not have much planned. Why don't we take a trip to Hedge Brooke and do some shopping? We can make it an overnight trip. We can find a hotel room for the night and rest up before coming home the next morning."

"Oh, Roger that sounds wonderful, but what about your work? Aren't you supposed to be close in the event you are called upon?"

"The Fort will get by without me for a day. Everything will be fine."

"That sounds wonderful then," she agrees.

"Stella is enrolling Matthew in school tomorrow and then she will be going to work. I want you to take the time while I am away and rest up. You are looking so tired. I do not want to wear you out on the trip."

"I will Roger, I promise."

Further down the Plains near the Lakota camp, Kikimo is out for a walk near the creek when he sees Rising Sun sitting next to the water with Sleeping Bear, who is now nine months old. He has noticed how isolated she has become since her father Red Hawk was killed and how overprotective she is of her baby brother from anyone who tries to help her with the care of the child. He has never paid much attention to Rising Sun, although he is not sure why, as she is not bad on the eyes. He comes down on the ground beside her. Immediately upon seeing him, she grabs Sleeping Bear in her arms and sits him down on her lap.

"I was not going to hurt him," he tells her.

"He is shy around others," she says.

"He would not be if you would allow him to be around others," he argues.

"He will have time when he gets older to be around others. Right now, I am all that he needs."

"There are many women in this camp that would be honored to help you."

"Song Bird provides enough food for him. I can give him everything else," she snaps.

"I have not come here to be quarreled at by a little girl," he barks.

"Then why have you come?"

"You have been different since your father died. You keep yourself and Sleeping Bear away from others. I am not alone when I say that I am worried about you. I thought maybe perhaps you wanted to talk."

"Why would I choose you, the Chief's son to open up to?"

"Because I know what it feels like to lose someone that you care about."

"You lost your birth mother many years ago, I am sure you do not even remember her."

"I am not talking about my birth mother. I am talking about Eagle Scout. He was like a brother to me."

"That hardly compares," she huffs.

"I understand now," Kikimo calmly says. "My loss is not as important as yours."

"Stop putting words in my mouth," she barks.

"My father was right," he says stomping to his feet.

"He is right about what?" she says.

"You are not my concern anymore," he snaps. "I have wasted enough of my energy on you." He is ready to storm off when he hears Rising Sun say. "Wait, don't go." He turns his attention to her and watches her remove Sleeping Bear from her lap and come to her feet.

"I am sorry," she tells him.

For a few moments, Kikimo just looks into her sad eyes. He can see under all that sadness that there is a beautiful girl who is strong and noble. She is a hard worker and takes on a great deal of responsibility, much more than other girls her age. He is uncertain as to why she has not completely been accepted by the others, or why his father has so much hatred for her. He actually feels kind of sorry for her and wishes she would warm up to him and stop being so hateful to him.

How exactly Red Hawk died is a topic that has been forbidden to be discussed by anyone in the camp. He himself only knows what his father has told him and he is certain that he has not been told everything. He is also certain that Rising Sun is in the dark as well.

"I am sorry that I called you a little girl," he says.

"That is alright. I am acting like one," she smiles.

"Has anyone told you how your father died?" he asks her.

"Just that the Chief killed him."

"Yes, he did."

"But why? Why would our Chief kill him?" she asks.

"My mother was there. I was not. She would know more than I do, but what I can tell you is I know my father. He is a peaceful man and he tried everything he could to have a peaceful outcome. Your father was a bitter man who had many skeletons and filled with a great amount of hatred for my father. Why, I do not know. I hear my father as he speaks to my mother at night when he thinks Little Foot and I are asleep on our pelts. I hear him tell her many things. He did not want your father dead and it pains him that he did what he did, but he had no choice, it was either him or Red Hawk."

"I always knew that my father disliked our Chief, but he never told me why," she says.

"Does it really matter anymore?" he asks her.

"Yes, it matters to me."

"Why, will it bring your father back?"

"Of course not," she snaps.

"Then let your father rest in peace and let it go."

"I cannot," she says.

"Do you not think that I wish I could go back to that day and change things? Maybe if I had done something different Eagle Scout and Flying Hawk would still be alive."

"What happened that day was not your fault."

" You are right it was not, just like your father's death was not yours. Standing there and asking yourself why and wondering what if is not going to bring him back or give him any justice. Your father was a lot of things, but he loved you and he would want you to move on. Just like I must move on without my brother, you must move on as well."

"But how?" she cries.

"You will find your way. The path will be open. Trust me Rising Sun, you will find it."

Rising Sun could not take it anymore and she starts to cry. She turns her head away so Kikimo cannot see her weakness. The gentle and kindhearted man that Kikimo has turned into, will not allow a woman to cry without being consoled. He comes up to Rising Sun and opens his arms up and embraces her as she weeps.

Evening falls across the Great Plains. I fall into a deep sleep with White Horse snuggled up next to me. I begin to dream. I dream that I am walking peacefully in a meadow, with White Horse. I am great with child. We are laughing and having fun. I am filled with peace and tranquility. I look up into the sky and the sun has disappeared leaving an eerie crimson color in the clouds. Vultures begin circling around me high up in the sky. A sudden fear comes over me. I feel an enormous amount of pain in my belly. I reach for White Horse, but he is not within my grasp. I am taken to my knees from the pain. I look down at the ground and it is filled with blood. I see a newborn lying within it. The child is dead. It is then that I wake up. My abrupt awakening has aroused White Horse and he comes up beside me. He immediately sees that I am shaken up.

"What is the matter my Love? What has frightened you so?" he asks me.

"Something is wrong." I answer him.

"What do you mean?"

"With the baby, something is wrong." White Horse starts to console me by rubbing my back.

"Why do say such a thing?" he asks.

"I saw it in my dream. We were walking together in a meadow. I am heavy with child. We are so happy and at peace. Suddenly, the clouds turn a dark crimson color and vultures appear high in the sky circling around me. I become fearful and I reach for you, but I cannot grab a hold of you. I am taken to my knees with the pain and fall into a pool of blood and inside the blood there is a baby and it is dead. It is our baby White Horse something is wrong with our baby."

"Oh, my Prairie Dawn," White Horse says, as he consoles me taking me into his arms. "It was only a dream. Our child is fine."

"How can we be so sure?"

"Because Medicine Moon is watching you," White Horse says. "If something was wrong, she would have told me."

"I do trust her. Her medicine is very powerful, but I would feel better if I could see Roger and have him check the baby out. I will rest more at ease."

"Sweetheart, your brother is a good hard distance away. I do not feel comfortable with you traveling at this stage. You are heavy with child. I will not chance your pony being spooked and you falling off of her."

"I rode when I was pregnant with Little Foot up to the day I delivered. I can handle a pony, as well as anyone else, especially my own," I argue. "Besides Roger even said he wanted to see me in a few weeks after we returned. If he did not feel it was safe for me to travel, he never would have wanted me to come."

"I will send Koawa to go get him," White Horse states. "You know him, he will ride hard to get here quickly."

I know White Horse means well and is only looking out for the safety of our child as well as me, but there is a very uneasy heaviness in me that is gnawing me away. I have to go see Roger.

"I cannot explain my reasoning of why I am so worried that something is wrong, but please White Horse, take me to my brother. We can take Medicine Moon along with us in the event that our child or I need something along the way."

White Horse can tell his Prairie Dawn is agitated about her dream and he feels that she is overreacting. His scouts have not seen any Blue Coats around here for several weeks and they have had no run- ins with any White Man for many months. He agrees with his wife that if Great Healer felt that she couldn't take the ride that he never would have told her to come. Although he is not real thrilled about his wife riding on a horse at this point in her pregnancy, he does not like to see her so upset. So, for those reasons, he will take her to her brother, so he can check her and the baby out and put her mind at ease. He will send his scouts out at first light to go ahead of them and clear out any potential danger that they may encounter along the way.

Stella is sound asleep in her small bed along with Matthew who is a short distance away. She is awakened from a deep sleep when she feels a hand come over her mouth. Her eyes turn big and her heart starts to pound with anxiety. The reflection of the moon through the small window is the only light that appears in the room. She tries to scream, but is quickly silenced when she sees the face of Blue Thunder. She is baffled as to how he got into the room. She is unaware of the secret passage opening behind the chest that leads to an underground fortress filled with gold. She is oblivious that that is how Blue Thunder got into her room undetected. After making himself known to her with his sweet handsome smile, he leans down and kisses her lips. Although she does not speak his language, it is clear to her as to why he is here.

"Matthew," she tells him, as she points to their son. He looks over at him and then back at her and smiles. In his tongue he tells her that it is alright. He is aware that she does not understand him, so he cups his hand around her face and kisses her again. After a few moments of putting her at ease, she gives into his advances and does not reject him anymore. She allows him to remove her nightgown from over her head and watches him disrobe himself. The love she had for this man all those years ago come rushing back to her as there lovemaking begins.

Chapter Four

The Pin

Roger is up just after sunrise to make the short trip into the Fort. He let his wife sleep and prepares his own breakfast and coffee before starting out. He noticed yesterday when he was driving his wagon home that it didn't feel right to him. He decides he will take the wagon into the Fort with him and have the blacksmith, Busby, take a look at it before taking it to Hedge Brooke this afternoon. He is ready to jump on it, when he catches Blue Thunder riding away over the hill. He pays little mind to it as he jumps on the wagon. He releases the brake and starts his ride to the Fort.

Very early in the morning, Grey Wolf located the slumbering Pawnee camp. He is crouched down in the tall prairie grass, along with the other warriors waiting to attack. He sees the opportunity and comes to a stand with his bow and arrow drawn. He then sneaks his way in with the other Lakota warriors and begin their sneak attack on the sleeping Pawnee village. It doesn't take him long to find the warrior who defiled Medicine Moon among the other Pawnee warriors, who are just starting to wake up and fight.

He ignores all the other enemy warriors, as he fixes his eyes on his target. He goes in for the kill and without much of a struggle he succeeds in bringing the menace down and collecting his scalp.

Eagle Moon is just as victorious clubbing a warrior to his death and adding his scalp to his collection, that is on his waistband. When Grey Wolf is satisfied with the success of the raid, he orders the retreat and the Lakota warriors head for home.

I have packed up my personal belonging bag and have it tied to my pony. I am giving her a quick brushing to her dark silky mane when my youngest son, Little Foot walks up.

"I want to go with you too Mama," he says.

"I know son, but your father and I both feel it is safer if you stay here."

"But Kikimo is going?" he argues.

"Kikimo is in training son and is scouting ahead with the others."

"But he still gets to see Leksi, Uncle Roger, and I want to see him too."

"Little Foot," I say. "This is going to be a quick visit. He is just checking on the baby and then we are turning around and heading back home. We will not be gone for long."

I hear Little Foot huff. I turn my attention to him and lift his chin. "I need you not to argue with me on this son, please. I promise you after your brother or sister is born and your Aunt Rose has recovered from giving birth herself, I will take you to see them. He is reluctant, but agrees to give me no more arguments.

"Are you ready my Love?" I hear my husband say, as he is coming up behind me.

"Yes," I answer. We quickly met up with Medicine Moon and Koawa who come riding up beside us on their horses. Although, I am fully capable of hoisting myself up onto my mare despite my big belly, White Horse lifts me up and places me on top of her.

"You behave yourself son and keep an eye on Morning Dove," I tell Little Foot. "We will be back sometime tomorrow."

"I will Mama."

With that said, White Horse jumps on his horse and on his command, we head out of camp.

Roger pulls up in front of Busby and brings his wagon to a stop. The burly blacksmith stops banging his metal and comes over to greet Roger.

"Good morning, Doctor Briggs," he says. "What can I do for you?"

"Wagon doesn't feel right to me when I go down a hill and it seems slow to brake," he says. "I was hoping you had time to check it for me. I am taking my wife to Hedge Brooke this afternoon for some baby shopping and would hate to have problems with it on the way."

"It will be a few minutes will that be alright?"

"I have some business to tend to," Roger says. "So, take your time."

"Come back in an hour," Busby says.

Roger grabs his medical bag from the back of the wagon and starts making his way through the Fort grounds. He knew he was not going to have any problems killing an hour and quickly finds himself a few patients to check in on. After an hour has passed, he starts making the short walk back to the Blacksmith. He passes a wood shop on his way and stops in front of the window when something catches his eye. He is so intrigued by it, that he decides to go inside and ask the shop owner the price.

"Good morning, Doctor Briggs," the man greets.

"Good morning," Roger greets back. "How much for that cradle in the window?"

The man walks over to the window and pulls out the cradle. He looks at the price tag that is hanging from it. It is marked five dollars.

"I am asking for five, but for you doctor I will sell it for three."

"Fine craftsmanship," Roger says examining the quality of it. "Definitely worth five dollars."

"You can have it for three," the shop owner says. "You tended to my youngster last summer for the price of a chicken. It is the least I can do."

"I have no problem giving you what it is worth, but my father always told me not to look at a gift horse in the mouth. I will take it." Roger reaches in his pocket and pays the man his money.

"Would you like for me to carry it out to your wagon Doctor?" the man offers.

"I thank you kindly, but my team is at the Blacksmith. It is a short walk from here I can carry it."

"As you wish. Please give my best to your wife. She must be due very soon here?"

"In a few weeks," Roger answers. "I must be leaving. Thank you again and good day."

"You too Doc."

Roger continues the short walk to the Blacksmith carrying the cradle in his arms as he goes. He is greeted by many townspeople and several offer to loan him a hand, but he declines and continues on his way. He stops short when he hears his name being hastily called from down the street. He turns around to see the young Corrine, the sister to the owner of the General Store. She is running down the walkway waving an envelope in her hand.

"Is everything alright?" he asks her.

"Oh yes, I saw you walking and wanted to catch you before you left. Will you give this to your wife please?" She hands Roger an envelope.

"It is an invitation for her to attend my tea party."

"Oh, alright," Roger says. His wife has been very isolated lately and is reasonably sure that she will not attend, but will give her the invitation anyways.

"It is crucial that she attend," Corrine tells him.

"I do not mean to sound rude," Roger says. "But Rose has been feeling poorly with fatigue and has been staying home resting."

"Stella has told us that she is isolating herself. You know as well as I do Doctor that that is not healthy. Why a woman in her condition should feel alive and radiant."

"Yes, I agree, but she is so great with child that she is uncomfortable. I appreciate the invitation and I will give it to her, but do not be surprised if she does not attend."

"She must attend! It is supposed to be a secret, so please do not tell her. All the women in the congregation are throwing her a surprise baby shower."

"Oh, how nice! She would love it."

"Yes," Corrine smiles. "So, you see Doctor, she has to attend."

"I will see to it that she attends."

"Thank you, Doctor." Corrine then notices that Roger is holding a baby cradle.

"Oh, how beautiful," she smiles.

"I think it is very nice," Roger says.

"Yes, it could not have gone to a better couple," she says.

"My goodness I must be running along I have more invites to deliver. Good day and tell Rose hello for me will you."

"Will do," he grins.

Busby is finishing up on the doctor's wagon. He found the problem and fixed it and is getting ready to hammer in the new pin when he hears a soldier approaching.

"You the blacksmith?" the man questions.

"Yea, what do you need?"

"My horse is lame. I need for you to check his shoe."

"Alright, I will be there in a moment."

"General Phillips needs it done now."

Busby hates to be told what to do. He is not one of the General's soldiers that can be ordered around, however he is in no mood to receive a lecture from the man in command, so for that reason he places the pin in the tongue and will come back to secure it when he is finished at attending the lame horse.

Roger has finally made his way to his wagon and sees his team hitched up and ready to go in front of the building. He places the cradle in the back of it and covers it with a blanket for protection. He looks around for Busby and notices that he is busy shoeing a horse. Roger sees that he has a new brake lever. He assumes that was the problem. He does not want to bother Busby and his trip to the Fort has taken him longer than he had planned. He is in a hurry to get back and pick up his wife and head to Hedge Brooke to get some shopping done before the sun sets. He will return tomorrow and pay Busby for his time. He is certain that Busby will be fine with it. He gets on his wagon, releases the brake and orders his team home, unaware that the pin that holds the tongue is not secured.

Further down the Plains, we have made it halfway to Roger's. White Horse stops us frequently, so I do not get overtired. Between Medicine Moon and him, I am staying well hydrated and nourished. We are going a little slower than I would like, but despite our slow pace we should still be able to make it to Roger's by nightfall. I still have this nagging feeling in my gut that I cannot ignore. I am feeling movement from the child within me. I am confident that my baby is alive in its womb, but something is not sitting with me and that is what is making me nervous. I am sitting on my knees near the water pouring some of it over my face to help keep me cool. I am joined by Koawa, who squats down beside me. He takes a sip of water before saying a word to me. "Are you alright?" he finally asks me.

"Yes," I answer.

"You sure? You have been awful quiet."

"I just cannot erase the feeling that is heavy inside me that something is wrong."

"White Horse told me your dream and why he has quickly decided to go to Great Healer."

"And you think I am being silly?" I ask him.

"No, not at all. White Fawn had many visions when she carried White Horse and I in her womb. White Horse and I both understand the power that a woman with child can have. That is why White Horse agreed to allow for you to go instead of me bringing Great Healer to you. You have the power to see what White Horse and I cannot. If you want to go to see your brother then we will go."

"Thank you Koawa," I grin.

"Get your fill of water, for very soon we will move on." He says, as he is coming to his feet.

Roger has made it safely back home and has Rose and himself packed up for the day trip to Hedge Brooke. They are making their way to the town with Max trailing behind them. To help the time go by, Roger starts a conversation with his wife.

"What do you think of the name Henry for a boy?" he asks her.

"Too country," she says.

"Well, he will be a country boy," Roger exclaims.

"Um, no he will not be," she teases.

"What about Winston?"

"Oh, heavens Roger, no."

"Well, what do you want?" he asks her.

"I like the name William. William Charles, now that is a very prestigious name. With a name like that he could be a doctor, a lawyer, why even the President of the United States."

"Well, I cannot argue with that," Roger admits. "And what about a girl? I have always liked Rebecca Elizabeth."

"Yes, I like that as well," she agrees.

"Well then it is settled. William Charles Briggs or Rebecca Elizabeth Briggs. I love it and I love you."

Roger leans over and kisses his wife. "I love you too," she smiles.

"I have been rather difficult lately and not easy to live with and for this I am sorry."

"No apologies necessary my dear. I understand how you feel. I think this trip is exactly what you need to boast your spirits."

"I will admit I am excited about it, even though it is only a short trip, it will feel so good to get away with only us."

Roger reaches for her hand. He gently kisses it. "I agree darling," he says.

The road to Hedge Brooke is hilly, but smooth except for the one rocky stretch when Roger will have to cross the shallow river to get to the other side. He has taken this trip many times and has never had any problems at crossing the river. As he nears the crossing point, he tells Rose to hold on as the wheels will hit many rocks making the wagon sway back and forth. She does as she routinely has done in the past and holds on as Roger crosses. Unbeknownst to them, the metal pin that holds the tongue in place begins to shake vigorously up and down with every turn of the wheels across the rocks. When the wagon hits the bank on the other side, it is then that Rose will release her hold. Roger will briefly stop until his dog has safely crossed. He watches Max shake his shaggy hair dry before continuing on. Hedge Brooke is less than two hours away.

The remainder of their travel is fairly quiet. Rose starts to nod off. Roger notices some Indian scouts off in the distance. A young scout wave down at him. It is then that he realizes that these are White Horse's scouts and that is most likely Kikimo waving at him.

He is not surprised to see his scouts, as he knows that he is in the heart of Lakota territory and White Horse's camp is only about a day's ride away. He waves back, as he continues on.

He is nearing the next hill where the incline going down is steep. He will soon be able to see how his new brake lever will hold up when he starts his descent down the hill. The metal pin in the tongue is dangerously moving up and down and ready to fall out. To his knowledge, he is having no issues with his wagon and sees no reason that he should not be able to push his team harder the rest of the way to Hedge Brooke. He hears his wife yawn and realizes that she is awake from her brief nap. He reaches over and squeezes her hand that is resting comfortably on their unborn child. His team is ready to make their way down the steep hill. At first all seemed well and he is having no issues. When the wagon starts picking up speed, he applies his brake to slow it down. Before he knew what hit them, the metal pin that is holding the tongue breaks free and the team of horses is off on their own. The wagon is going so fast down the hill that all Roger has time to do is brace him for the inevitable. He hears Rose scream as she goes flying in midair. He then himself goes airborne when the wagon begins to roll. There is an eerie stillness in the air when the wagon comes to a stop and the still bodies of Roger and Rose lay on the prairie grass.

Chapter Five

The Lost Soul

Blue Thunder has caught up with the other scouts at a watering hole. Kikimo is allowing Spirit Dog, the army horse that he received last Christmas from his Uncle Roger, to drink. He notices a dust cloud high in the sky close to where he just saw his uncle. He points it out to Blue Thunder.

"It is in the direction of Leksi, our Great Healer," he says. Blue Thunder agrees.

"We have to wait for the Chief, but we will go and leave the others here to investigate." Blue Thunder says.

Kikimo along with Blue Thunder leave the other scouts behind and start to make their way to the other side of the hill.

Further down the Plains, we are making great time and should be at Roger's very soon. We have had no delays and have not seen any signs of any Blue Coat's along our way. I am growing tired and White Horse wants to stop again, but we are so close that all I want to do is push on.

We are traveling across the open Prairie. The air is unusually hot for this time of year and I fear we are in for a hot and dry summer. My bladder of water that I have tied to my horse is nearly empty. I know of a watering hole that is between Roger's and Hedge

Brooke where White Horse is heading. There, we will meet up with our scouts who will take us the remainder of the way to Roger's and we will be able to allow our horses to drink and fill up our water supply. We are only a few miles away from it and should be there shortly. As we heading in the direction of the watering hole, I look up at the sky, it is then that I get a cramp in my stomach and hear in my head the scream of a woman. I flinch in pain, as I hold my stomach. Medicine Moon looks over at me.

"What is wrong Prairie Dawn?" she asks me in her tongue. Upon hearing this, both White Horse and Koawa look my way. The pain subsides as quickly as it came.

"Just a little cramp. I am alright. It has passed," I answer her.

"We need to stop," White Horse says.

"No White Horse, I am fine. Really, I am just a little dehydrated with this afternoon heat and my water bladder is empty."

White Horse then removes his water bladder from around his waist and hands it over to his wife.   "I think we need to stop. You have been riding a great distance today, you need your rest."

"No honey please," I plead after I take a drink. "We are only a few hours away. I can make it. I promise you I would tell you if I couldn't. I too wish no harm to our child."

"I will not allow you or our child any harm, we will stop," he argues.

"Sweetheart, I understand you are concerned for me and our child, but it is silly to stop now when we are so close."

White Horse understands his wife's desire to move on, and will usually accommodate her wishes, but this time he insists that she rest for a little while before moving on.

"We will stop here and you will rest," he tells her.

"White Horse," I begin to argue. He holds his hand up to silence me. "We speak no more of this," he tells me. "You will rest."

I know it is pointless to argue with him any further. When White Horse has made up his mind he is like a bull, trying to get him to change it.

Roger wakes up to one hell of a headache and a pain in his leg. It takes him a few seconds to comprehend what has happened. He rubs his head and notices that he is bleeding from it. He looks around at the wreckage scattered all around him, it is then that he remembers Rose. He staggers to his feet, as he is holding his head. He is feeling a little off centered and his leg is heavy with pain, but he is determined to find his wife. He notices his dog Max, sitting near the overturned wagon. The dog barks at him. It is then that his heart skips a beat when he sees the lifeless body of his wife pinned under the tongue of the wagon.

"Rose," he mumbles, as he quickly staggers over there. He reaches for a pulse and is relieved to see that she has one. Although his head is pounding and oozing out blood and the pain in his leg is excruciating, he puts his own injuries aside to help his wife. He tries to lift the tongue from the wagon off her, but quickly realizes his own injury has hindered his strength. He assesses her wounds and attempts to arise her awake. She fails to move. He then starts to worry about the baby, as the tongue is lying directly on her abdomen. He tries again to move the tongue. Even a half of an inch would help her. He again fails. He slides himself down on the ground beside her in total despair. He has never felt more helpless in all his life. His head is throbbing. The blood that is seeping out of it is starting to trickle down his cheek.

He looks down at his leg and can see through his pant leg that it is bleeding. Although he cannot be certain of how badly he is injured, he believes that nothing is broken. He reaches for Rose's hand and again tries to wake her by calling out her name. His emotions are building when she fails to move. He hears horses approaching and he hears Max bark. He looks over just as he sees Blue Thunder and Kikimo riding up. Kikimo is the first to jump off his horse. He runs over to his uncle. He backs up when Max starts growling. The dog is clearly in protection mode and does not want Kikimo or Blue Thunder anywhere near them.

"He is confused and protecting," Blue Thunder says. Blue Thunder reaches into the pouch around his waist that is holding some dry meat, he tries to calm the dog down by offering him the meat and softly speaking his tongue to him. With Blue Thunder distracting the dog, Kikimo runs up to Roger.

"Leksi!" he exclaims. Roger has never been so relieved to see his nephew. He starts to cry.

"Oh, thank you Jesus," he says. "You came." It is then that Kikimo sees Rose.

"Oh Leksi," he gasps.

"I can't get it off of her," Roger says.

Blue Thunder has managed to calm Max down enough that he is no longer concerned of getting bit. He is quick at reacting and with the help of Kikimo, they both move the tongue off Rose. Roger is immediately by her side and he is in a panic when he notices that Rose is bleeding profusely from between her legs. Despite his pounding head, Roger knows that this much blood can only mean one thing. His wife is hemorrhaging. He has no time to waste.

"My medical bag," he cries out. "I have to find it. It has to be around here somewhere."

Kikimo and Blue Thunder scatter around to try to find it. Blue Thunder finds it in the prairie grass not far from the wreckage. He runs it over to Roger. He then speaks his tongue. Kikimo does the honors of translating.

"He said that our Chief is close and he has your sister and Medicine Moon with him. He is going to them and bring them back here to help. I will stay here with you until they come."

"Rose," Roger says. "She is hemorrhaging. I have to remove the baby from the womb." Kikimo looks at him in horror.

"Leksi, are you sure?" he asks.

Roger takes a heavy sigh. "With this much blood, I fear our child is dead, and if I do not stop it my wife will be too."

Kikimo can see how upset his uncle is becoming. He puts his hand on his shoulder.

"I am here for you Leksi," he says. "Just tell me what to do."

Roger reaches into his medical bag and pulls out what he needs. His leg throbs with every movement he makes and his head is still oozing blood, but he pays no attention to his medical needs and puts all his focus on his wife and unborn child. Kikimo watches his uncle pour some liquid into a rag. He then hands it to him.

"Even though she is not awake," Roger begins. "Put this over her nose for a few seconds every few minutes. As much as I want her to wake up, now would not be a good time."

Kikimo does as he is instructed and makes sure that Rose stays under as Roger begins. He watches his uncle's hands start to tremble, as he tries to make the incision. Kikimo places his hand on top of Roger's. Roger looks up at him.

"You can do this Leksi," Kikimo says. With that said, Kikimo guides his hand along with Roger's to keep it steady, as his uncle makes the incision. They hear Rose moan. Kikimo is quick at placing the rag over her mouth and putting her to sleep.

Blue Thunder has made it to the watering hole. He quickly discovers that his Chief and the others have not yet arrived. He tells the remainder of the scouts what has happened. Several of the scouts race off to help Kikimo, as the remainders join Blue Thunder in finding their Chief.

Upon seeing his warriors running in hard, White Horse is certain that something is wrong. We are all on alert when Blue Thunder stops his pony in front of his Chief.

"Great Healer and his wife have had an accident," he tells White Horse in his tongue. "Kikimo is with them. His wife is in a bad way."

"Oh my God," I gasp.

"Where are they?" White Horse asks.

"A few miles from here," Blue Thunder answers.

"Quickly everyone, mount up!" White Horse orders. White Horse then turns to me. "I know you will not stay back with your brother in trouble," he tells me. "You stay as close as you can, I will be riding fast."

"Go, White Horse!" I tell him. "Medicine Moon and I will catch up." With that said, White Horse is off in a hard run, with Koawa and Blue Thunder right beside him.

Roger removes the dead baby from its womb, moments before he hears Max bark and a swarm of warriors coming in. He chokes back his emotions as he hands his dead child to Kikimo, who is waiting with a blanket that he found in the wreckage of the wagon. A warrior by the name of Black Feather comes down beside Kikimo. Together they look down at the baby boy.

"I am so sorry my little one," Kikimo whispers to him. He folds the blanket around the baby and gently places it on the ground beside him.

Black Feather looks over at Roger. No words are spoken by the mighty warrior, but Roger can tell that the man is sympathetic and showing compassion. He watches Black Feather come to his feet and start to walk away speaking his tongue to the remaining warriors.

"He told them to start collecting things from the wreckage to make a shelter for you and Rose," Kikimo says. Roger faintly nods his head, before turning his attention back to his wife. He finds a tear in the uterus. It is beyond repair. He is faced with a decision that will affect his wife greatly. If he is to save her life and stop the bleeding he must remove the uterus from her, which will make her sterile forever. But if he does not remove it, he knows that she will bleed to death. He wastes no further time on his decision and does what he has to do. He is quick at removing the uterus which stops the bleeding. He is just finishing up on closing her up when he hears

Max bark again. He then sees White Horse with his warriors coming in hard. Kikimo rushes over to his father, just as White Horse is jumping off his stead.

"I am so glad you are here Father," he tells him.

"Me too," White Horse says. He hurries over to Roger, coming down beside him. Roger has finished with Rose. He is sitting beside her in a daze holding his dead son in the blanket. White Horse places his hand on Roger's shoulder.

"The tongue of the wagon," Roger begins, "rolled onto her and the weight of it caused her to hemorrhage. She lost the baby. I had to stop the bleeding. She would have died if I hadn't. I didn't have a choice. My wife will forever be baron."

"There is nothing more that you could do for your wife right now," White Horse says. "There is a shelter being gathered and my warriors will build it over your wife. Come my brother and let me tend to your wounds."

"I have to bury our son," Roger cries. White Horse squeezes his brother-in-law's shoulder. "There will be time for that. First, we need to take care of you. Kikimo can sit with Rose, we need to get you cleaned up."

White Horse removes the baby from Roger's arms and gently hands it to Kikimo, who lays it down on the ground near his mother. White Horse then helps Roger get to his feet. The depth of his injuries begins to surface when Roger stumbles as he comes to a stand. White Horse notices his hurt leg and calls for Koawa for help at getting Roger to some shade under a nearby tree. He is tending to Roger's head, when he sees his wife and Medicine Moon coming in.

As I am dismounting my horse, I take a quick look around at the overturned wagon and the contents of it scattered across the prairie grass. I notice Roger sitting nearby next to my husband, who is tending to my brother's head. Near the overturned wagon I see a makeshift shelter and Kikimo sitting underneath it. My stomach immediately does circles as I know that this is bad. One of our

43

warriors spots me as I dismount my horse in the event that I should fall. He then takes my horse's lead when he knows that I am stable and walks away. I rush to meet up with my husband. Medicine Moon, who is carrying her medicine bundle of herbs, joins Kikimo under the shelter.

"Roger," I gasp, as I come down beside him. It is clear to me upon seeing my brother that he has suffered some injuries due to the accident. Despite his head that is still oozing blood, I notice one of his pant legs is torn and his leg looks quite swollen and has a deep gash in it. He appears to be in a daze and in his own world. I am not certain if this is due to his head injury, or the initial shock of the accident. I touch his shoulder. It was enough to bring Roger around.

"Carrie," he says.

"What happened?" I ask him.

"The tongue of the wagon," he begins, "came off. I lost all control of the team. The wagon rolled and both Rose and I were thrown. The tongue had her trapped and the weight of it was on her stomach. She started to hemorrhage. I had to stop it, or she would have died. Our baby did not survive."

"Oh Roger," I console. "I am so sorry. How is Rose?"

"Her uterus was torn. I had to remove it, or she would have died. I need to go to her."

"Kikimo and Medicine Moon are with her. She is in good hands."

"I want to be with her when she wakes up."

"Roger, you are hurt," I tell him.

"I want to go to her." Roger looks over at White Horse.

"Please help me get over there," he begs him.

With the assistance of White Horse, Roger makes it back over to the wagon and down to Rose. Medicine Moon has already completed her herbal treatments on her and is sitting beside her when we arrive.

I come down on the other side of Rose. It is then that I see a blanket that is neatly folded around something. I am certain that it is the baby. I have to see it for myself. I start to pick it up. White Horse holds my hand back.

"No, bad medicine," he says.

"What?" I question.

"You are with child, you are bringing bad medicine onto it by holding that baby," he explains. I look at White Horse in disbelief. He places his hand onto mine.

"I understand he is your kin and your desire to hold it, but you must understand that you could bring bad medicine to you and our child if you allow yourself to hold it."

I have lived with the Sioux long enough and know how powerful they believe that their medicine is. I personally feel that White Horse is being a little overprotective. I have always accepted his beliefs and have never questioned them no matter how far fetch some of them may sound, so for that reason I do as he wishes and as painful as it is for me, I leave the baby where it lies. I look across at Roger. I have never seen him so distraught. It is important that I am there for him, as he is going to need all the emotional support that I give him. I suck in any emotions that I am having and remain strong for my brother.

Early evening has come upon us. White Horse has sent his scouts further out to detour away any unwelcome travelers, or soldiers, that may stumble upon us. Although we are not on the main path that most would take to get to Hedge Brooke, it is a path that is known by mountain men and Blue Coats. Being that we are very close to the Fort, White Horse is keeping his scouts on guard. Tomorrow morning a travois will be built for Rose and we will take her and Roger home. But for tonight, we will remain here and allow both of them to rest.

Koawa went hunting for us a few hours ago and brought back a buck. Kikimo left to get us enough water for the night. Blue Thunder left along with White Horse the find our scouts and station them for the night. This makes Koawa temporarily our only protection until they return. Koawa is skinning the deer and I am cooking up the meat as he is tossing it to me. I look across the fire and see Roger approaching. Earlier, Medicine Moon applied some of her remedies on Roger and wrapped his leg and head. Koawa found him a branch that he can use as a walking stick for support. He is getting around better and is holding up very well considering what he has been through. He finds a place across from me and sits down.

"Is she still asleep?" I ask him.

"Yes," he answers. "But she is showing signs of coming around. I think she will be awake soon. Medicine Moon is sitting with her. I needed some fresh air." I hear him deeply sigh. I look across the fire as I flip the meat over and see his long, drawn face.

"I don't know how to tell her that our child is dead and that she will never have anymore. She has always wanted a family. She is not going to take this well."

"Do you want me to tell her?" I ask.

"No," he declines. "It should come from me."

"You had no choice, Roger. You did what you had to do to save her life."

"I am not sure that she will see it that way." I watch Roger remove his glasses and rub his eyes and then place them back on.

"We went on this trip to spend some time together before the baby was born and pick up some things for it. I just took that wagon in this morning. I had a new brake lever put in. I do not understand what happened. I have taken this trip a thousand times. I could go down that hill blind folded. I do not understand how that pin came out."

"Roger it was an accident," I tell him. "You did nothing wrong. It was a cruel sense of nature. I am just thankful that our scouts were so close. I shudder to think what could have happened if we did not get here as quickly as we did. It was just a freak coincidence that we here."

Just then we hear Medicine Moon speak her tongue, as she quickly races to us.

"Rose is waking up," I tell Roger.

Roger is quick to his feet and races the best that he can to his wife's side. The makeshift tent that is shielding Rose is covered with a thin layer of canvas that was taken from the wagon. She is far enough away that we cannot hear what Roger is saying, but no words need to be said, when we hear Rose cry out, "No!" and starts to wail. My heart goes out for her. The amount of pain that she must be feeling has to be unbearable. I fight my own tears back, as I hear her grieve.

Chapter Six
The Empty Soul

The reflection of the full moon radiates high in the evening sky. White Horse and Blue Thunder left on horseback a few hours ago to try to track Roger's horses and bring them back before we leave in the morning. Our scouts are stationed nearby and will remain on their guard through the night. Roger and Rose have fallen asleep. Medicine Moon and I are taking turns sitting with them. It has been a very long and emotional day and I am feeling very drained. I have found a spot under a lone tree, just at the edge of the camp on a hill. I have been here for a few minutes in prayer and relaxation. Koawa has returned to camp from his evening patrol and sees me through the reflection of the moonlight. I watch him start making his way to me. He squats down beside me.

"Are you alright?" he asks me.

"Yes. It is a lovely night. I thought I would sit here and enjoy the evening breeze."

"I agree that the night is beautiful, but you need to come back down by the fire."

"Why?" I wonder.

"You and Kikimo need to stay near the fire and not stray away from camp without me."

"You worried about Blue Coats?" I wonder.

"No, our scouts will keep them away."

He reaches for my hand to help me to a stand. I have known Koawa for as long as I have lived with the Lakota and he and I are extremely close. I notice he appears to be a little uneasy and keeps glancing out into the darkness around us as he is talking to me. This is very unusual behavior for a man who fears nothing. Koawa has a bizarre ability to smell danger before it arrives and it has saved his life on numerous occasions. I see him inhale some of the evening air and then quickly grab my hand and pull me to my feet.

"To the fire, now!" he orders. I am now feeling a little on edge and I can feel my heart starting to race.

"Koawa what is it?" I ask him in a panic.

"Shungkmanitutonka," he says.

In Lakota that means a big dog that hunts walking or better known as a wolf. Immediately my heart jumps into my throat. No sooner had he said that than we see the wolves circling in. Koawa quickly has me shielded next to the tree and is facing the angry wolves head on. The Alpha of the pack is just inches from us and is the boldest of them all. Fear enters my soul, as I am certain that at any moment Koawa and I are going to be attacked. Suddenly, we hear a gunshot and the wolf's scatter. I look into the darkness and see White Horse approaching holding his rifle.

"You two alright?" he asks.

"I must say my brother," Koawa says. "As always your timing is amazing."

"You should not be this far away from the camp," he barks.

"It is my fault White Horse," I tell him. "Roger finally went to sleep and it was such a beautiful night that I thought I would sit under the tree and wait for your arrival. I had no idea that the wolves would come in this close."

"They smell the blood in the air and the distress from the accident," White Horse says. "Koawa picked up their tracks when he was out hunting. I knew they were close. That is why Blue Thunder and I left to go find Roger's horses before the wolves got them."

"Did you find them?" I wonder.

"Yes, they were not too far away. Blue Thunder has them tied." As White Horse is talking to me, he is looking over at Koawa.

"I am sorry White Horse. Koawa was taking me back when the wolves arrived."

"I am sure he was," he says. "The wolves will not return tonight. You will be able to rest freely. Go back to camp now."

"Are you coming?" I ask him.

"I will be there in a minute," he answers.

I do as I am told and make my way back to the fire alongside Kikimo. Koawa starts to walk away.

"You stay away from my wife," a jealous White Horse warns.

Koawa turns around and looks at him.

"If it weren't for me, your precious wife would have been that packs dinner." With that said, Koawa turns around and walks away.

The morning sun is upon us. White Horse is eager to move us on and take Roger and Rose home. Rose has been sedated by Roger and is sleeping peacefully on the travois that is fastened to the back of White Horse's pony. He offered to make one for Roger as well, but Roger refused stating he is strong enough to ride.

Another travois was made that will carry what belongings that could be salvaged from the wreckage and taken back home.

Medicine Moon, Kikimo, and I, are collecting what we can that is scattered across the Prairie. I come to a sunken part of the grassland and glance down. I spot something lying in the bottom of it. I make my way down the short dip of the land to see what it is.

"Oh," I cry, when I notice it is a baby cradle. It has significant damage to it that is beyond repair, but I start collecting the broken pieces of it on the ground anyway. My heart begins to shatter, as I think of the loss of the child that the cradle was meant for. I am so lost in my thoughts and my grief that I fail to see White Horse come up beside me. He sees the broken pieces of the cradle in my hands and he hears me sniffling. He places his hand on my shoulder.

"This is the meaning," I tell him.

"The meaning of what?" he asks me confused.

"The meaning to my dream," I answer him. "Medicine Moon even told me that my dream was not for me and she was right. It was for Rose. It was her baby that I saw lying dead in the pool of blood. It was her scream that I heard in my head. It was not our baby that was dead, it was hers." I turn into his chest. "It is just not fair, White Horse, it is just not fair."

Our conversation is interrupted when we hear riders coming in. White Horse and I make our way up the incline, just as we see Grey Wolf and his war party riding in.

"I see many scalps hanging on my warrior's spears," White Horse says pleased. "There will be much celebration when they get home."

"Why are they here?" I wondered out loud.

"I am sure they ran into our scouts and were told what happened. They will see us home."

As White Horse and I are walking to join Grey Wolf, I see Medicine Moon rushing over to him. It was not long after that when we head for home. Roger finds a crate that was not too badly damaged in the accident and uses it to lay the baby in to take home for burial. He has it safely secured on the travois next to Rose. When everyone is in place, we head for the short journey to Roger's home.

Several hours pass. Stella is cutting up fresh vegetables in a bowl and Matthew is playing with a toy next to the fireplace.

"We will eat shortly son," she tells him. "Why don't you go to the stream and wash up."

"Aww, do I have to?" Matthew whines.

"Yes, you have to to." She answers. "Now no fussing, go do as you are told." Matthew fails to move. "Now go, hurry along." She shushes him off.

"Fine," he huffs, laying his toys on the floor. He makes his way to the door, when it suddenly flies open.

Stella jumps at the sudden burst of the door opening. Her heart skips a beat when she sees Rose draped across Koawa's arms and Roger leaning on White Horse.

"Oh, my word," she gasps. "What happened?"

I am the last one to walk in, following close behind Kikimo.

"There was an accident with the wagon," I begin to tell her. "Rose was seriously hurt."

Koawa finds his way to the bedroom and gently places Rose on the bed. White Horse helps Roger at sitting down in the chair beside her. Stella grew deathly still, when she looks down at Rose's stomach and notices that she no longer has a child in it.

"Oh my God," she gasped. "What can I do?"

"I am going to need some fresh water," Medicine Moon says in her tongue.

"Stella," I translate. "Can you get some fresh water please?"

She is quick at leaving the room and going to the kitchen area to grab a bucket. Matthew is cowering by the fireplace, unsure on what to think of everything going on around him.

"Matthew sweetie," Stella says. "Why don't you come with me to the creek and help me get some water."

The boy is quick at reaching for his mother's hand. Stella spots Blue Thunder. They exchange a smile before she walks out the door.

The morning rises across the Prairie. There is nothing more that we can do for Rose. Time is going to have to heal her wounds, that I am sure are very deep and swollen inside her. Roger is slow moving. Although I know he is hurting both physically and mentally, he pays little attention to his own wounds and remains focused on his wife. Today Stella is going to go take the short ride to the Fort and relate to General Phillips about Roger's accident. She is then going to go to the post office to send a message to Rose's mother in Boston.

It is time for us to leave as well. I really do not like the idea of leaving Roger, but I know if we were to stay that we would only be in the way. I give my brother a hug and head for home.

Chapter Seven

The Visitors

Several days pass. Upon receiving the word of the accident from Stella, General Phillips is quick at visiting Roger and offering him whatever support that he can. He also gave Roger a generous amount of personal leave time to be with his wife and mourn the loss of their child.

Upon hearing the terrible news, Busby could not help but feel responsible for the accident. Roger holds no fault on him and has assured him that there are no hard feelings. Busby, feeling like he had to do something, took it upon himself to bring a wheelchair from Roger's clinic, so Rose can at least get out of bed. Roger wants to bury their child, which they named William, next to his father in Willow Creek, but because of the distance of Willow Creek, being nearly a month away, he has decided to bury him under a big spruce tree near the creek bed. Rose is still weak from her surgery, so with the aid of the wheelchair he pushes her the short distance to the graveside. She distraughtly listens on, as Roger speaks a few phrases from the bible over their son's grave.

Stella is in the meadow picking flowers. Lately she has been spending a great deal of her day away from home. Although Roger has never made her feel unwelcome, this has been a difficult time for him and she feels it is best to keep her distance until things settle down. Her work for the General's wife is not as steady as it was at first. She feels it is because of Matthew. He has become the gossip of the Fort. He is darker skinned and has thicker features than any of the other children and many are questioning why. She hears the rumors that she was once an Indian whore or had taken up with a Mexican outlaw. Unfortunately, Matthew has to take the brunt of the teasing with the other children, this angers her but there is little that she can do, as she holds no weight in the town and refuses to go to Roger for help. Her thoughts are interrupted when she hears movement behind her. She quickly turns to see Kikimo and Blue Thunder.

"You gave me a start," she gasps.

"We are sorry. We did not mean to frighten you." Kikimo says. "We saw you from a distance. You have been sitting here for some time. Blue Thunder wanted to make sure that his Rose Petal is alright." She grins over at him. Just to look at him makes her insides tingle.

"I am alright."

"How is my Leksi?"

"Leksi?" she questions.

"My uncle," he clarifies.

"Oh, he is fair."

"And my aunt?"

"Her heart is in a lot of pain."

Kikimo is saddened to hear this. "She just needs more time. I will ask my spirits to find peace in her heart," he says.

"Thank you," she mumbles.

Blue Thunder speaks his tongue.

"He is asking how Little Fox is."

"Who?" she questions.

"Matthew," he answers.

55

"He is doing just fine. Little Fox is that what he calls him?" she asks.

"Yes, it the Lakota name that he has given him."

"That is so cute," she smiles. Blue Thunder softly speaks his tongue to Kikimo.

"He wants you and Little Fox to come to camp tonight."

"Are you sure I am welcomed?"

"You are one of us now. You will always be welcomed."

She looks over at Blue Thunder. She would be absolutely crazy not to go with him. She walked away from him once and she is refusing to make the same mistake again.

"I would love to come." Kikimo translates to Blue Thunder. Stella watches him as he grins. He speaks his tongue.

"He will meet you both here tonight just after sundown."

"Alright." The men turn to leave.

"Kikimo," she says. He turns around to look at her.

"How hard is it to learn your language?"

"For the ones who do not want to understand, it is very difficult."

"Can you teach me?"

"Yes, I can teach you." With that said, he turns and quickly catches up to Blue Thunder.

The afternoon sun is high on the Plains. Roger is preparing him a cup of tea. His mind is heavy on his wife. Physically she is healing very well, but her emotional scars are very deep. She is very bitter towards him and has made it clear how angry she is with him for making her sterile. He has tried numerous times to explain to her that he had little choice in the matter and if he had not made the decision that he did, that she would have bled to death. Still, this does not seem to matter to her as she shrugs away any of his comfort or support. His thoughts are interrupted when he hears a knock on the door.

"Corrine," he says, after opening the door.

"Hello Doctor Briggs," she says sweetly. Roger is confused as to why Corrine would make the ride out here and can only assume that his services are needed back at the Fort.

"General Phillips has given me a generous amount of time off. I understand that he has called in another physician to temporarily take my place until then…" She interrupts.

"I have not come to render your services," she says.

"Oh, I beg your pardon," Roger says. "I just assumed."

"With the high afternoon heat and the distance, one must travel to get here, I can clearly understand why you would think that," she says.

"Then forgive me for being so curt, but why are you here?"

"I am here to see Rose."

"That is very kind of you and I know you have come a long way, but Rose is not up for company."

"I am not company I am a sister of her congregation and I am here for support."

"Corrine," Roger begins.

"Doctor Briggs, I know what happened and I know how heartbroken she must be. I have the rest of the women from the church coming over. They should be here very shortly. I know how important Rose's appearance is and I wanted to allow her time to get herself presentable. Please, allow me in."

Roger faintly smiles. "Maybe another face to look at that isn't mine would do her some good. Come in." Roger walks Corrine back to the bedroom. Rose is lying awake in bed.

"Sweetheart you have company," Roger says. Rose looks their way. Her eyes are vacant, heavy and distraught.

Before Rose can refuse, Corrine is by her bed and starts up a conversation right away. Roger closes the door behind him, just as he hears another knock on the door. He opens it up to a herd of women anxiously waiting to come in. He is greeted by each one of them and presented with comfort food and condolences. The women find Corrine and Rose in the bedroom. Corrine steps out just as Roger is putting the basket of bread that he just received on the shelf.

"You look exhausted," she says.

"I am a little," Roger admits.

"These women can talk for hours and I am not doing anything this evening. Why don't I stay with Rose and give you a break?"

"I don't think I should leave her," he argues.

"Now I may not be a doctor and I have never had a child or a husband, but I think I have a pretty good idea on how she is feeling as well as you. You need time away, Doctor. Do you have some where you can go for the evening?" Roger knew of a place and he needed to check on his sister anyway.

"Yes, I know of place."

"Then it is settled," Corrine says. Roger faintly smiles.

"Thank you, Corrine."

She is ready to turn around when it occurs to her. "Stella is still staying with you, correct?"

"Yes," Roger answers.

"And her boy, what is his name again?"

"Matthew."

"Yes Matthew."

Roger is aware of the hostility that is going on with Stella and Matthew. He is about ready to defend them when Corrine smiles over at him.

"Good, I hope we see them."

Stella arrives home just briefly enough to change her clothes and check on Rose. Corrine was nice to her and encouraged her to stay, but Stella quickly declines, stating she has other arrangements and disappears with Matthew upstairs.

"Other arrangements," Molly smirks. "I can just imagine what they are." A few of the other ladies laugh.

"She really is not that bad," Rose says.

"Rose it is clear that you are not in your right mind," Molly smiles. "I need to tell your husband to cut you back on the sedative." Several of the other women laugh.

Upstairs in the very small loft, Stella can hear the comments and laughter down below. She is buttoning Matthew's shirt, as she bravely attempts to ignore the hostility towards her down below.

"Mama, why don't the church ladies like us?" Matthew asks.

"Because we are different," she says.

"How are we different?"

"Because we just are," she says. "Now go put on your boots, we have to meet up with your father."

"Hooray I get to see father!" he excitedly yells.

"Matthew hush, remember we are to tell no one who your father really is."

"I know if I was to tell it could get us and father in big trouble."

"That's right," she agrees. "Now hurry it will be sundown soon and we still have a little ride ahead of us."

"Yes Mama."

Kikimo and Blue Thunder are waiting under a tree for Matthew and Stella to arrive.

"There they are," Kikimo says in his tongue.

Blue Thunder steps out from under the tree and waits for them to approach. Matthew waves over at his father. Blue Thunder reaches up in front of Stella to lift Matthew off. Matthew has taken a liking to Kikimo and is quick at running over to him to greet him. Blue Thunder reaches up to lift Stella off the back of the horse. He fixes his eyes on her and for a few moments neither one of them blinks. He gently kisses her forehead, before putting her down.

The bright circle of the moon lights up the Lakota camp. A fire is lit just outside our lodge. White Horse is joined by our company around the fire and everyone is finishing up there evening meal.

Matthew and Little Foot have become very good friends and are practically joined at the hip. With their bellies full, they run off to play nearby. Blue Thunder nudges Stella to follow him.

"The meal was delicious," she says to me. "Thank you."

"You are welcome," I say. With that said, she reaches for Blue Thunder's hand and together they disappear into his lodge.

"Young love," I say.

"Age does not matter, when it comes to the fondness of the heart," White Horse smiles over at me.

"I remember when you and I were like that," I comment.

"We still are," he says. "My love has not changed for you just because we are older and married."

"You know what I mean," I smile.

"I know that the child that you are nurturing in your womb is made from love. The same love that we had when we made Little Foot."

White Horse is right. If anything, our love for each other has become stronger over the years. I cannot imagine my life without him. I reach across and place my hand onto his. I am ready to kiss him when we hear riders coming in. Through the darkness we see the riders come into view. It is Grey Wolf, Eagle Moon and several other scouts riding in for the night and with them they bring a visitor with a dog.

"Roger?" I say bewildered. "What is he doing here?" I wonder out loud. Soon my question will be answered as we watch Roger hand off his reins to Kikimo and head our way.

"My brother," White Horse says. "It is good to see you. Come join us." Roger takes a seat next to me. Max finds his place next to White Horse.

"What brings you here at this time of night?" I ask him as he reaches over to give me a hug.

"I needed some air," he says.

"Your heart is heavy," White Horse says.

"Yes, I am sorry if I come at an inconvenient time."

"You are always welcomed," White Horse says. "Are you hungry? I can have one of the women make you something to eat."

"No, thank you."

Roger is not the kind of man who shares his emotions, he never has been. He is a lot like my husband in that matter. But I can see the emptiness in his eyes, the sunken sadness that is written all over his face.

"What is matter?" I ask him.

"A few of the church women are at the house to cheer Rose up. One of them is staying with her tonight so I could get away."

"How is Rose doing?"

"Physically she is healing well, but mentally she is angry. She won't talk to me. She barely even looks at me."

"Her heart is still aching," White Horse says.

"We buried our son near the creek. I go and visit him every morning. I ask her if she wants to go along and she refuses. She sits in our room most of the day just staring out the window. She refuses to eat. I have tried talking to her, but all she does is blame me for our son's death and her being sterile. I do not know what else to do. No medicine that I have will heal her broken heart."

"Many storms shall come and go as the seasons pass the land, so shall sorrow also pass," White Horse comforts.

"I am not so sure White Horse," Roger says. "She is hurting so deep. I don't know if she will ever get over this."

"Before you leave tomorrow, we will go into the sweat lodge and ask our spirits to show you the way."

The evening dwindles away and everyone scatters to their lodges. Roger finds a spot between Kikimo and Little Foot for the night. It does not take long for any of them to fall asleep.

Chapter Eight
The Doe

It has been seven days since Roger stepped out of the sweat lodge. Things have only grown worse with Rose. She has become more distraught and bitter towards Roger. She rejects whatever sympathy or affection that he may give her. He is trying to remain patient with her and give her whatever time she needs to heal her heart from their loss, but his patience is running thin. Today he decides that he has had enough and will confront her about it. He finds her in the bedroom sitting in the chair. He sits down on the bed beside her. She fails to look his way or even give any acknowledge that he is in the room.

"Rose, I spoke with Reverend Abrams this morning. He feels that we would benefit from some counseling. He feels if we both just sit down and talk about our loss that we could…"

"What does he know about loss!" she snaps.

"He is a man of God. He knows how to preach to someone the value of a loss."

"I have not lost a puppy, Roger," she barks. "My baby is dead and thanks to you I will never have the chance of having another one."

"I lost a child as well. Have you forgotten that?"

"I could care less how you feel. It is not your body that has been mutilated. I have not only lost my son, but I will never be able to know what the feeling is like to hold a child in my arms."

"Rose, darling I know how it must feel."

"Do you?" she roars. "You never wanted children."

"That's not true," he argues.

"Isn't it?" she snaps. "You never have time for me, why would I think you would ever have time for a child."

"Do you think that I made you sterile on purpose, because you think that I do not want any children?"

Rose huffs and turns her head away.

"Just leave me alone Roger. I can't stand the sight of you right now."

Roger is beside himself. Never has Rose talked to him in such a way. He stares at his wife for a few seconds before coming to his feet.

"I have taken the liberty of wiring your mother in Boston. We both agree that you need to go there and recuperate. Staying here only allows you to live within the hurt. You can stay as long as needed. I will send you money every week."

She fails to look at him, but nods her head in agreement.

"I have you scheduled on the stagecoach tomorrow morning. You need to get your belongings ready that you wish to take with you."

He begins to walk out the door and stops to address her one last time.

"I love you Rose, but what you are doing to us is not healthy and I will not support it. I did what I did to save your life and I will not apologize for that." With that said, he walks out the door.

Stella is spending more and more time away from the cabin. If she is not working at the Fort, then she is with Blue Thunder, either at his camp or somewhere in the wilderness. On one visit with Blue Thunder, she runs into White Horse and tells him what is going on with Roger and Rose. Feeling that his presence may be needed, he leaves with a few of his warriors to Roger's home.

I am due to deliver at any time. Because of this, I do not stray far from camp and am never left alone when I do. Today, with White Horse and Koawa away, I leave the short distance away from camp with Medicine Moon to collect berries and herbs for her medicine bundle.

"The Great Spirit has come to me," Medicine Moon begins, "they have told me that your time is very near and I should stay close to you."

"You are sounding like my husband," I tease her.

"He is only concerned about you, as am I. I am glad that he is bringing the Great Healer back. I fear that you are going to need him."

"Why?" I wonder, "You have born many babies. Mine will not be any different."

Before she can answer, I spot a familiar root on the ground.

"When the time comes," I tell her. "This is the root that I need to control the bleeding."

"I am aware of this," she says. "They sprout abundantly this time of year. My Chief and I have everyone marked so when the time comes, we can collect them quickly."

"See, you have everything under control," I reassure her.

We continue at a slow pace collecting herbs and berries. We are walking alongside a low bluff that overlooks the river. Medicine Moon is my protector, as well as my best friend. She is a female version of Koawa. So, seeing her glancing around from time to time gives me no alarm, as Koawa does the same thing.

"How are you and Grey Wolf doing?" I ask her.

Before she answers, I suddenly see her whip out her knife and Night Eagle the warrior appears. Before I have the chance to look behind me and see what has her so alert, she pushes me off the bluff and into the river below. After a few seconds I surfaced, stunned but uninjured. I look up at her on top of the bluff and see her just as she finishes killing a mountain lion. It was then that I realized that this thing was following us and got too close for comfort and Night Eagle pushed me out of the way before it attacked me.

I make my way out of the water and onto the shore. She yells down at me.

"You alright?"

"Yes," I yell back. "Next time warn me, will you?"

"Sorry, there was no time, he was right behind you."

I look around for a way to get up to her. The landscape is very rocky and steep.

"I am going to have to find another way up. This is too steep and I am way too pregnant to climb it."

"Alright, I will meet you."

"Don't toss the cat," I tell her, as I start climbing the incline, "We can haul it in and have the meat for dinner."

"Alright," I hear her yell. "Just be careful, I don't want you falling."

"It is alright to push me six feet into the water though," I tease.

"Sorry," I hear. Her voice is sounding more distant.

This time of year, the foliage is thick, as are the bugs. I swat some away as I continue. I am uncertain exactly where I am at, but I can hear and smell the river and know the camp is in front of me. I call to Medicine Moon, Night Eagle! I hear nothing. I wonder if she is having the same problem as I am.

I have been walking for a good while and really starting to get tired. I find a tall tree and sit underneath it for a bit to catch my breath. I look around to see if anything looks familiar, but it doesn't. I am no longer able to hear or smell the river. I know for certain that I am lost. I am convinced that camp has to be nearby. I look at the side of the tree and find the moss. "Perfect," I think to myself. "I am heading the right direction." Just then I hear rustling in the bushes. I wonder if it is Medicine Moon. I look that way and see a doe step through the trees. She stops and looks at me. I thought this was odd, as most deer will run away when they know that they have been spotted. For a few seconds I just watch her. The doe fails to move.

I decided that my break is over and it is time to move on. I hold my tummy as I come to my feet. I expect the deer to run off as soon as she sees me stand, but she doesn't even flinch. I glance back at her as I start to walk again. I am perplexed and a little baffled when the doe starts to follow me. I make it a few steps when I am hit with a hard contraction. I bellow in pain and am quickly bracing myself on a tree trunk until it passes.

"Oh no," I cry out, when I feel a warm wetness between my legs. I look down at the ground and panic when I see that my water has broken. Just then I am hit with another contraction. It is then that I am certain that I am in labor. I come down on the ground and lean up against a tree. I notice the doe is standing nearby.

Further in the woods, Night Eagle is in a state of great anxiety because she cannot find Prairie Dawn. She made it down to the river where she pushed her in and back tracked back up through the woods where she saw her last. She looks up at the sky and sees that the sun is past its highest point and concludes that she hasn't seen her in over three hours. She is less than two miles from camp and wonders if Prairie Dawn found her way back on her own. She knows her soul sister is very familiar with the woods and is confident that she made it back on her own and is probably resting on her pelt until she returns. She turns around and hustles back to camp to catch up with her. She will come back with her pony and pick up the mountain lion later. She will bring Eagle Moon with her to help her lift it.

I am certain that the camp is nearby. I come to my feet and start to walk again. I keep an eye on the moss on the trees to make sure I am heading in the right direction. The doe is still with me. For some reason the doe feels as if she needs to stay with me, almost as if she is protecting me or guiding me.

My walk is going slow and my contractions are continuing. I have walked less than half a mile in about two hours. I am exhausted and cannot walk any further. I am certain that Night Eagle is looking for me and the longer it takes her to find me the more anxious she will become. I decided to just stay here and let her find me.

I am going to have to start preparing for the inevitable, as I am certain that birth is not far away. Building a fire is the first thing that I must accomplish. I have to be able to boil water and start preparing the root before my contractions are so close together that I am unable to move. I am too far from the river to gather more water and am going to have to use the water that I have in my water bladder around my waist and just pray that it will be enough to boil the root. As painful and as exhausted as I am, I come to my feet and find what is necessary to start a small fire.

Night Eagle has made it back to camp and quickly rushes into Prairie Dawn's lodge, only to see that she is not there. She rushes around camp looking for her. She sees Eagle Moon near the river.

"Have you seen Prairie Dawn?" she asks him.

"I thought she was with you," he answers.

"She was until we got separated when I pushed her in the river."

"You pushed her in the river?" he asks confused.

"Yes, a mountain lion was following us, and it was getting too close to her so I pushed her into the water so it wouldn't kill her and then I killed the lion. She was making her way back to me. Something is wrong. I must go and find her."

"I will go with you," he says.

"No, Grey Wolf is out scouting. Go find him and tell him what has happened. Tell him to start looking by the bluff. She can't be far."

"She is near her time," Eagle Moon says.

"You think I am not aware of that. Now go! Daylight is wasting."

Night Eagle quickly finds her horse and rushes off back to where she last saw Prairie Dawn.

White Horse is on his way home with his brother–in–law, who he convinced to return with him. With Prairie Dawn near her time to give birth, it did not take much convincing for Roger to come. They are making great time and in the home stretch.

I have a small fire burning near me and have the root boiling in some water. "58, 59, 60, 5," I count out loud. "Five minutes," I say. My contractions are five minutes apart and growing in strength. I am now very concerned, as I know I don't have much more time. Between the contractions I watch the doe. She is the only company I have right now. I have lived with the Sioux long enough to understand their beliefs and culture. The Sioux believe that every person has an animal spirit that guides and protects them. I have never really understood this and at times thought it was strange. If I had not witnessed this firsthand, I would probably still be a skeptic. The way that this doe is acting I am certain she is here as my protector and I am welcoming it. She has not moved from the nearby grass which she has been sitting on for several hours.

Night Eagle has made it back to where she last saw Prairie Dawn and starts tracking her further into the woods. Her tracks are fairly fresh which makes her think that she is not behind her by much and that Prairie Dawn is either moving very slow or is not moving at all. This concerns her, as even in her condition she should be moving much faster and should be a considerable distance ahead of her and should have made it back to camp before she did. She fears that Prairie Dawn is injured or even worse and has gone into labor. "Great Spirit, take me to her," she mumbles to herself.

White Horse and the others have made it back to camp. Eagle Moon is quick at telling his Chief what has happened.

"Grey Wolf and Medicine Moon are out looking for her now."

White Horse rushes off along with Koawa and Roger to help in the search.

Night Eagle is concentrating on the lay of the land and looking for any tracks or clues to which way Prairie Dawn may have gone. She spotted something in the grass. She kneels down. She runs her fingers through the moistness of it and smells it. "Her water broke," she says to herself. It is then her worse fears come to life Prairie Dawn is in labor.

I let out a bellow, as my contractions are coming in hard. I just barely catch my breath before another comes. My hips feel like they are breaking. I look over at the doe. She has moved closer to me and is standing fully upright. I close my eyes for a split second to catch my breath and when I open them the doe is gone. It was just moments after that when I see Medicine Moon running up to me.

She is quick at assessing the situation and becomes horribly concerned when she lifts my dress to examine and sees the babies heel. She knew she needed help. She sees the root boiling on the fire nearby. She rushes over to the fire removing the root and building the fire higher. It wasn't the safest route to go as the smoke could be seen by the enemy as well, but she is left with no other choice. Prairie Dawn needs help and fast. She knew it was just a matter of time before it arrived.

White Horse and his warriors are frantically searching. He is certain that she cannot be far away, as she would not have left camp but more than a few miles in her condition. He sees a flat part of the prairie grass leading into the woods. He spots a Doe standing on top of the hill looking down at him. He thought this was odd. He watches the doe turn to walk away and then it stops, looks at him and then turns again almost as if the doe wanted him to follow her.

"This way," he tells them. He quickly makes his way up the hill and stops when he sees the smoke. He points. "There," he says. Everyone then sees the smoke.

"That has to be her," Roger says.

"Carrie wouldn't let that smoke get that high unless she was in trouble. We must hurry." White Horse says.

The ring of fire is upon me and I am wanting to push.

"No Prairie Dawn," Medicine Moon says. "Don't push."

"I have to," I pant. "I have to push."

"No Prairie Dawn the baby is stuck."

"What do you mean stuck?" I pant.

"I can see its foot."

Before I can respond I am hit with the worse contraction yet. I bellow out in pain. Just then White Horse and others come racing up. White Horse is off his horse before it even stops and is running to my side. Roger is close behind and quickly at my legs.

"Carrie," White Horse says.

"White Horse the baby is breech," Roger says.

"What is that?"

"It means the baby is feet first."

"Is that bad?"

Roger looks up at me as I cry out with another contraction.

"I need to push." I cry out.

"No Carrie!" he says. "Whatever you do Carrie, do not push."

White Horse is beside himself when he hears his Prairie Dawn crying out in pain.

"Medicine Moon support her head," Roger orders. He then looks over at White Horse. "You are not going to like me."

"What are you going to do?" he asks.

"I am going to try to turn the baby and Carrie this is going to hurt, but if we do not turn the baby it will strangle on the cord."

"What can I do?" White Horse anxiously asks.

"Get the root ready because once I do the baby will come fast."

"I am not going to leave her," White Horse snaps.

"White Horse!" Roger snaps. "You want to help your wife then get the root ready."

Koawa pulls White Horse back and takes him to the fire to prepare the root. His heart goes heavy when he hears his Prairie Dawn screaming in pain as Roger turns the baby around. He then hears Roger say. "Carrie push." He waits a few moments and then he hears the cry. His child is born. He grabs the root and runs back to his wife.

"Carrie," he says stroking my hair.

"White Horse," I faintly smile. He leans down and kisses me.

"I want to see the baby," I say.

Roger hands the infant to Medicine Moon and then turns his attention back to me. Medicine Moon hands me our daughter.

"She is so beautiful," I cry.

"Like her mother," White Horse grins.

"I am sorry White Horse," I tell him. "I didn't mean to get lost."

"You never mind that," he says kissing my hand. "I am just grateful that you and our child are alright."

"White Horse she is bleeding pretty heavy," Roger says.

"Darling," White Horse says. "You need to drink the root."

"The doe, where is the doe?" I ask.

"Sweetheart," he coaxes as he places one arm behind my head so I can comfortably drink "I want you to drink." I do as I am instructed.

"Slow drinks," Roger says.

"Where is the doe?" I ask again after I swallow.

"What about the doe?" White Horse asks

"There was this doe that stayed with me the entire time. I have never seen anything like that before."

"There was this doe that I saw when I arrived," Medicine Moon says. "She pranced off when she saw me. Returned a few minutes later and sat a few yards away until she heard you and then she left."

White Horse smiles, "You my love," he says, "just saw your animal spirit. In our custom when you see this animal that is the name that you are to give your child."

"Doe," I mumble to myself. "Yes, White Horse that's it.

Prancing Doe. We will name her Prancing Doe."

It was then that I became very weak and things started to turn black. Medicine Moon removes the baby from my arms. Roger looks across at White Horse with great distress in his voice. "She is losing too much blood White Horse," he says.

"We will get her back to camp," White Horse says,

"She should not be moved White Horse she is very weak," Roger argues.

"She is not safe here. Wolves will smell the blood and attack. Camp is only on the other side of that ridge I will carry her. There she will drink more tea and rest."

I remember very little from the trip back home. I fell limp in my husband's arms as he was carrying me across the plains. Medicine Moon has Prancing Doe safely secured in her arms wrapped in some swaddling clothes. We head into camp and all eyes are on us. Minoke is quick at rushing up to her Chief and holding the flap open to our lodge so he can step in. He lays me down on our pelt and covers me up. The baby is placed in her crib beside me.

"For now, my Prairie Dawn and my Prancing Doe will rest," he tells everyone.

With that said, White Horse comes to his feet swishing everyone out except for Medicine Moon and Roger. There I would lay to regain my strength and for the bleeding to stop for the next three days.

Chapter Nine

The Mysterious Man

Three days have passed and it is late afternoon. Prancing Doe and I have been resting in our lodge. Kikimo and Little Foot have both held their little sister and have made a bond with her that will last a lifetime. Word has spread around the camp on the arrival of our child. I have been showered with gifts and blessings as everyone shows their love to the Chief's daughter.

Both Roger and White Horse are concerned about me having too many visitors in my weakened state and has only allowed Medicine Moon to stay with me. This saddens me, because I miss all the other ladies and have enjoyed their company, but I give my husband no complaint and remain in my lodge. Thank goodness for Medicine Moon and the caring of a new infant to help pass the time.

I am resting on the pelt that I share with my husband watching Roger, as he examines Prancing Doe who is lying on a pelt beside me.

"Is she alright?" I ask him.

"She is strong and healthy," he smiles. "Although I cannot be certain without the proper scale, but if I had to guess I would say she weighs around seven pounds."

"She is Lakota, and White Horse's daughter, I would expect her to be very strong."

"We just have to watch her, as I have seen a baby be born strong and then deteriorate within the weeks, because they are not getting enough milk."

"I never had problems producing milk with Little Foot. I do not see any reason as to why I would with her."

"Every child is different Carrie," he says. "And times are different now. Food is harder to come by and you are not eating like you used to when you had Little Foot. I will keep an eye on her weight and yours over the next few weeks."

I smile over at him. I could not help but wonder if he was like this with all his new mothers, or if he was being over cautious because he is her uncle and my brother. Either way I was glad he was here.

I know the last few months has been horribly hard on him with him losing his own child in that terrible accident and then Rose leaving for Boston on such bad terms. My heart went out for him. As much as he loves being a doctor, I think taking some time away from it and being around loved ones is the best thing for him.

"Have you heard from Rose?" I ask him.

"No, I have sent her several posts and I have had nothing in return. I have thought of going to Boston myself just to make sure she is alright, but afraid it may just make it worse."

"If you want my advice," I say. "I would give her a little bit more time and see if she will come back on her own."

"Is that what White Horse would do?" he grins.

He knows as well as I do that White Horse would come after me. It would be a cold day in hell before he would allow me to stay away. Before I could answer him, we heard a commotion outside. I perk up.

"Something is wrong." I said, "Could be Blue Coats."

"It is too quiet to be Blue Coats. I will go check it out. You just rest. I will be back shortly."

When Roger steps out, he spots Koawa and Grey Wolf riding in. On the back of Koawa's horse is a warrior draped over its back. Roger watches White Horse and several other warriors approach them. Koawa lifts the warrior off the horse and carry him to a nearby tree, where he lays him down. Upon seeing this, Roger quickly grabs his medicine bag and rushes over there to see if he can be of some sort of assistance.

"We found him a few miles back lying in the grass," Koawa says.

The man is unconscious and bleeding from his abdomen. Roger is quick at applying pressure to the wound, as he feels around for the extent of the injury.

"It has missed anything vital," he says. "The wound is not too deep."

"So, he will live?" White Horse asks.

"He appears strong and in good shape. I will clean him up and treat his wound. He will be alright."

"Good, because I need to talk to him," White Horse says. "I want to know how he got his injuries. If he was found only a few miles away, we could be in danger if his injuries were given to him by Blue Coats." White Horse looks over at Grey Wolf.

"Take a party and go scout further out. Keep a watchful eye. Report back if you see anything."

"Yes Chief." With that said, Grey Wolf rushes off.

Roger tends to the warrior and allows the man to sleep. He then returns to his sister and niece.

Evening is fast approaching. Although I am feeling stronger, White Horse wants to keep me in for in our lodge for another day. As much as I am itching for fresh air, I know better than to argue with him.

White Horse sits besides his wife cradling his daughter, as his Prairie Dawn eats.

"Our daughter has the skin of a Lakota but like her brother, Little Foot has the eyes of her mother," he says.

"I see a lot of you in her as well," I state.

"She has Lakota in her blood, that is from me. Everything else is you." He smiles coming down on the pelt beside me. He glances over at my dish. "You are eating better today. I am happy to see that."

"Yes, Roger says I am doing well. Tomorrow, I want to go to the creek and bathe."

"That will be fine. I will have Medicine Moon go with you."

He turns and holds Prancing Doe like a football in front of him. "She needs to be cleansed as well." He then stands handing her to me. He leans down and gives me a kiss. "But for now I need both my ladies to get some rest."

White Horse removes my plate and hands it to Medicine Moon who has just entered in. "Make sure she rests," he tells her before exiting the lodge.

White Horse watches his warriors conversing around the campfire. He takes the small walk to the injured warrior sound asleep under the tree. He looks down at him. He can tell he is Sioux. His mind is twisting and turning. He cannot stop thinking about this warrior. Who is he? Why was he alone? Where was he going? And how did he get injured?

He worries that it may be Blue Coats, because he has not seen or heard much from the men in blue for several months. Now that Roger is away from the Fort, he is not able to keep tabs on them. This makes him very nervous, because quiet soldiers are never good. His thoughts are interrupted when he sees the man move. He greets the man with a grin, as he opens his eyes.

"Welcome back my friend," he greets him. "I am Chief White Horse." White Horse squats down in front of the warrior. "And may I ask who you are?"

"Chief White Horse, you are the man I have come to seek."

"Who are you?" White Horse asks again.

"I am Spotted Bear. I was sent along with our war party by our Chief. He needs to speak with you."

"Why did he not come himself?" White Horse wonders.

"He is frail and does not travel. He said he knows you well and was certain you would come."

"I know every Chief around here and all their warriors. How come I do not know you?"

"My Chief is Little Elk. I am his nephew. My father is…"

"Charging Bull," White Horse answers.

"Yes."

"How is your father?"

"He passed on last winter from fever."

"I am sorry for this," White Horse says. "I spent many sun dances with your father. He was a good man. I have sat in council with your Chief. You were always away whenever I came. There is one thing that I do not understand though. How did you get injured?"

"Our party was ambushed by soldiers. I got away because I outsmarted them. I found your camp. I was nearly here when the pain was so intense and the bleeding so thick that I collapsed."

"You will rest. When you are strong enough, we will go see your Chief. Until then, I will have our Great Healer come and see you and we will bring you food."

"Is that who put these bandages on me?"

"Yes. You are very lucky. He said you will survive." Spotted Bear dozes back off to sleep.

Several hours would pass and a cool evening breeze covers the Lakota camp. Roger comes down to the sleeping warrior and pushes the blanket free from his chest so he can better access his wounds. Spotted Bear awakens and sees a White Man over him. His eyes turn to ice, his body becomes stiff. His muscles begin to bulge. In a flash he reaches up and grabs Roger by the throat and squeezes. Roger gasps for air. Upon hearing the struggle with Roger, Koawa and White Horse are quick at coming to Rogers's aide and peel the tight gripped hands of Spotted Bear off Roger's neck. Spotted Bear spats in his tongue, while Roger gasps for air.

Koawa is quick to Roger's side, as White Horse glares over at the injured warrior.

"That man saved your life and this is how you thank him?"

"No White Man will ever touch me," Spotted Bear spats, as he spits on the ground. "White men are liars. Spotted Bear kills all white man."

Spotted Bear then lunges at Roger knocking him backwards to the ground. Koawa is quick at coming to Roger's aid. White Horse steps between him and Roger. He glares down at Spotted Bear.

"The only way you will ever get to this man, is through me," he warns.

"Little Elk said you were a wise man. What would he think if he knew you are actually a fool!"

White Horse is a very patient man, especially with his own kind, but he was not taking kindly being called a fool by a man who he could have left for dead on the prairie grass.

"It is because of Little Elk and you are injured, that I will sit back and let you insult me. But let me assure you, if the situation was any different the pain that you are feeling right now is nothing to what I can do." White Horse squats down in front of Spotted Bear, "I am sure Little Elk has shared in his council my reputation on what I can do to people who defy me."

Spotted Bear is aware of this Chief's perseverance when it comes to fighting the enemy and his reputation of being very brutal.

"If you wish no aid from this Great Healer then that is on you. I will see that you are fed and that a lodge goes up for you. I will provide you with your own horse. You are free to come and go as you wish, but one thing I will not allow is any harm to come to that man. If you so much as look at him wrong I don't care who your kin are, I will kill you."

With that said White Horse comes to his feet. He reaches his hand down and helps Roger to his feet and then together they leave Spotted Bear where he lays.

Well into the evening White Horse returns with some food for Spotted Bear. He places it down on the ground beside him and squats down in front of him.

"I understand you wish to speak to me," he says.

"Yes, I was hasty with my words to you earlier. My father would not be happy with the way I spoke to a Chief."

"You are lucky I am in a good mood," he says. "What is it you wish to speak to me about?"

"My Chief, I do not know what it is Little Elk wishes to speak to you about, as he did not share and I did not ask, but he made it very clear to me that he needs your assistance."

White Horse thinks a moment. There is something about this request that is just not sitting right with him. He knows Little Elk very well and knows he is a kind man. He also knows that he can be a foolish one as well when it comes to hiding from the enemy. His camp has been raided twice within a year from Blue Coats, the last one killed nearly everyone in his band and has left him with few warriors. He is wondering if maybe this has something to do with it.

"We will go," he says, "when you are healed enough to ride."

"I can ride Chief. Your Medicine Man can help me."

"The same Medicine man you tried to kill," White Horse says.

"I was wrong. I know what the Blue Coats did to your wife. I helped in the search to find the men who did it. I know you did not put your mark on the White Man paper because of it. Your hatred for the White Man is great, so for you to trust him then he must be alright."

White Horse is still a moment. The man's words have a lot of truth in them and Little Elk warriors did help in the search for the two Blues Coats who raped and beat his wife two summers ago, but there is still something about this man that White Horse doesn't trust.

"Alright I will allow it."

He motions for Koawa, who is standing by the center fire watching his Chief very carefully to come over and to bring Roger with him. As the men approach White Horse comes to his feet.

"I'll be close," he tells Roger before leaving them alone and joins Koawa around the fire.

Roger is quick at doing what needs to be done. He can feel the warriors' eyes are thick on him and it is making him nervous. Although White Horse is only a stone throw away, he feels very threatened. He hears the man grunt when Roger examines his ribs. He briefly looks up at him. The warriors' eyes were as black as marbles and very intimidating. He reaches into his medical bag to grab another bandage. Then he hears the man speak.

"Are you his hostage?" he asks. Roger is taken back a little at the man's English words.

"No," he answers. "I am free to come and go as I please."

"Why do you come?"

"Because I want to be here," Roger says.

"No, why they want you here?" Spotted Bear asks.

Roger is not sure where his questions are going and not sure he wants to stick around and find out. He has finished cleaning his bandage and closes his medical bag and stands up.

"The Chief is a friend of mine." Roger answers.

"How you met friend?" Spotted Bear asks.

"He came to me a few years back. He needed White Man medicine."

"Hmm," he hears him grunt. Roger does not like the way that this man is looking at him and he is starting to get nervous.

"Chief is good at staying ahead of the soldiers," Spotted Bear says. "Makes man think how he does that?"

Roger looks down at the warrior very puzzled by his odd comment. "I wouldn't know," he says and walks away.

Roger leaves the warrior where he sits and quickly approaches White Horse who is sitting by the fire with a few of his warriors. "We may have a problem," Roger says.

"What sort of problem?" White Horse asks.

"How well do you know that warrior?"

Not well," White Horse answers. "Why do you ask?"

"He spoke to me in my tongue." White Horses ears perk up. "He said something to me that I thought very odd. He said the Chief is very good at staying one step ahead of the soldiers and is curious as to how that could be."

"That is odd," White Horse agrees.

"White Horse I think that warrior knows more then what you believe he does. His wounds are superficial and not too deep. He could have done it himself. He was not shot, he was stabbed. Army does not stab people."

"My brother, you underestimate me," he grins. Koawa chuckles. "I know his wounds are not from a gunshot. His wound is from a lance that is similar to the one I have in my own lodge. As just before you arrived, I was telling my men that something is not correct with this man who calls himself Spotted Bear and we need to watch him."

"White Horse I am afraid if you leave with him, you may be ambushed by the soldiers. I know they have Indian scouts and I know many of them can speak my broken tongue. The General thinks you are dead, but he knows that your band is still out here and he is determined to find you."

"Relax my brother. I too have thought of this. Tomorrow Koawa will move the camp and Grey Wolf and Eagle Moon will join me and we will go to Little Elk's camp. I know exactly where his camp is and I know for a fact that his Chief is not frail."

"Then why are you going?"

"Because my brother, I too love a good game." Both White Horse and Koawa laugh.

Chapter Ten

The Betrayal

It is first light and Roger leaves for home. I tried to convince him to stay and move with us to our next camp, but he says he has stayed long enough and he must attend to some work at home. I am concerned that his mind is not in a good place and his heart is broken with Rose leaving him the way she did. He never had proper time to grieve the loss of their child and I fear it is starting to get the best of him.

I have seen very little of Blue Thunder. I was beginning to get concerned for him, until Grey Wolf told me that he saw him and the White Woman camped out near the stream not far from here. I am certain that it is Stella and she is staying with him while Roger is gone and Matthew is at school.

White Horse left at first light with Eagle Moon and Grey Wolf to go to Little Elk's camp with Spotted Bear. White Horse is minimally armed and only has two warriors with him which concerns me if in the event he runs into Blue Coats. He also told me that he would not be gone for very long. Which I find odd as well, as I know Little Elk's camps is a good distance away.

Prancing Doe and I had a cleansing done this morning in the river. It is custom three days after giving birth for this to be done. I had it done when I had Little Foot as well. I am feeling so much better and Roger is alright with me starting back to my daily routine as long as I can tolerate it.

I am kneeling at the stream alongside Minoke, washing a few dishes, before starting to pack up for our move in a few hours. Prancing Doe is in her papoose sound asleep beside me. I glance across the water and notice Kikimo wading his feet in the water next to Rising Sun and Sleeping Bear, who is sitting on her lap. They appear to be having an enjoyable conversation. I catch Kikimo stroking Rising Sun's cheek. I deeply sigh, as I fear he is starting to have feelings for her.

"I do believe the Chief's son is smitten with her," I hear Minoke say in her tongue. No one here except for Koawa, knows that Rising Sun is White Horse's illegitimate daughter and he wants it to stay that way.

"Yes, I see that," I sigh.

"Do not worry," she says, "in just a few months Kikimo will be of age. He will go on his vision quest to seek his name. Rising Sun has already had her first flow. She is no longer a child. They will be together. The spirits will make it so."

I know Minoke was trying to put me at ease, if she only knew why this could never be. Just then I hear Prancing Doe start to fuss.

"She is getting hungry," I say out loud.

"Go feed her, "Minoke says. "I will finish up here."

"You sure?"

"Yes," she answers.

"I will send Morning Dove to help you finish up." With that said, I lift the papoose and make my way to my lodge.

Further down the Prairie, Blue Thunder has set up a small camp nestled in the trees near a stream. He makes his way up a small hill carrying firewood, as Stella starts to prepare the duck that Blue Thunder hunted earlier that day. He comes down on his knees and drops the wood beside her. He then starts to build the fire. During their time together, when they are not making love, they are teaching each other their language. Although Blue Thunder is not as quick at picking up the English language, she herself has picked up enough words and has been taught enough sign language that their communication is getting better. As she is picking off the feathers from the duck, she glances up and catches Blue Thunder staring at her.

"What?" she blushes.

"Marry me," he says.

"Your English is improving," she smiles. He reaches for her hand and gently pulls her over to him. She stops the task at hand and follows his lead.

"Marry me," he says again.

"You are serious?" she says. He didn't understand. So, she signs it.

"You are true on what you say. You want me to marry you."

"Yes," he says in his tongue.

"Matthew will have his father all the time."

"We have more, many more," he grins.

She blushes. She has been with many men during her past life as a prostitute, but she has never been more fulfilled and received more joy during it then when she is with him. Her feelings for this man are like nothing she has ever felt before. She wants to spend each and every awaking moment with him. For the first time in her life, she has felt loved.

"Yes," she says. "I will marry you and I will have many babies with you."

His smile was wide with joy. He is so much in love with his Rose Petal. He whisks her in his arms and passionately kisses her. For the moment the food and the fire were going to have to wait, as Blue Thunder was hungry for something else.

White Horse and his men have been riding for hours. He has been staring at Spotted Bear for most of the ride, trying to get into his mind. He does not believe his story on Little Elk being frail and needing to speak to him, as he just had council with Little Elk a few weeks back and he was fine. He did not get much sleep last night due to his mind doing circles and what he was going to do if his suspicions are correct.

He loves playing cat and mouse games with the enemy, but he is concerned about Roger. If he isn't careful Roger could get into some serious trouble of even killed. This is something that would devastate him and he would never hear the end of it from his Prairie Dawn.

He glances over at Grey Wolf and motions for him to come up alongside of him. White Horse then leans over and quickly signs to him. Grey Wolf then stops to wait for Eagle Moon to catch up to him and repeats the sign to him. Spotted Bear is in the lead and looking ahead and does not notice what is going on behind him.

Another hour would pass and it is nearing the time when they will have to turn east to the home stretch to Little Elk's camp. Spotted Bear cannot believe how easy this has been and how quickly the Chief agreed to come along. The surprise that the Chief will receive when he rides right into the Army's trap. The Chief will have no chance to escape. He is thankful that he was able to convince Little Elk to move his camp two days ago and even more grateful that the General agreed not to attack their camp anymore in exchange for getting the leader of the band that has been a thorn in his side for months.

Spotted Bear grins to himself at how careless and eager the Chief is to only bring two puny warriors with him for protection and the Chief is not even carrying a gun on his horse. He laughs to himself at how gullible he is as he always thought the Chief was a wise man. His thoughts stop when he sees the Chief stop between two large boulders next to the watering hole.

"Chief," he says in his tongue, "Little Elk's camp is very close, the horses will be allowed to rest and water there."

"Horses are thirsty, we rest." White Horse says.

Spotted Bear gets off his horse, followed by Eagle Moon and Grey Wolf. He watches the Chief lead his horse to the water and follows along to lead his. Grey Wolf circles in behind Spotted Bear just when Eagle Moon grabs Spotted Bear from behind and puts a knife to his throat. Spotted Bear tries to break free, but Grey Wolf kicks him in the stomach. White Horse then towers over Spotted Bear. "Now I am only going to ask you once," he says, "Who sent you to my camp?"

"I told you Chief Little Elk needs to speak to you,"

White Horse looks over at Grey Wolf and nods his head. Grey Wolf elbows him in the groan. Spotted Bear bellows in pain. Eagle Moon grabs him again in a choke hold and presses the blade of the knife into his neck.

"Do not lie to me!" White Horse roars.

"I am not Chief. I swear I'm not."

"Do I need to remind you who you are talking to and what I do to men who lie to me?" he barks.

Eagle Moon presses the knife further into Spotted Bear's neck. Spotted Bear knows he does not have a chance at fighting them off, so he tries to bluff his way through.

"Alright, alright," Spotted Bear says.

White Horse nods his head to Eagle Moon to release his grip. Spotted Bear comes to his knees gasping for air. White Horse looks down at him.

"Tell me now."

"I don't know why Chief Little Elk wants to talk to you. Maybe because he knows you are a snake when it comes to hiding from the enemy," he lies.

White Horse's patience is gone. He squats down in front of Spotted Bear and in a flash grabs one of his fingers and breaks it. Spotted Bear cries out in pain.

"If I have to take you out piece by piece I will," he growls. "Now I am not asking again, who sent you?"

"I told you my Chief Little Elk wants to speak with you."

A very inpatient and angry White Horse breaks another finger. Spotted Bear bellows in pain.

"You want to keep going?" White Horse asks, "because when all your fingers are broke then I will start with your teeth."

Spotted Bear sizes up his competition. He looks up at Eagle Moon and Grey Wolf and has realized how badly he underestimated their strength. White Horse stands up and when not getting a quick enough response he nods his head at Eagle Moon. Eagle Moon then has his knife at Spotted Bear's ear.

"Your last chance or the ear comes off."

Spotted Bear's eyes are filled with fear. He looks across at Grey Wolf and then at the Chief. White Horse nods his head at Eagle Moon to go ahead.

"Okay," Spotted Eagle whines, "I will tell you."

"Very wise of you," White Horse says.

"The General at the Fort paid me to find your camp. He told me to come up with the story to get you to Little Elk's camp."

"Why?" White Horse asks.

"To kill their leader. I convinced Little Elk to move the camp. The General promised that he would not attack our camp anymore and would provide us with rations if I would help him locate you and lure you in."

"Why?" White Horse growls.

"He is certain that someone from the inside is helping you. His reputation is on the line, as you are making him look like a fool. He is waiting at Little Elk's camp to ambush you. I stabbed myself and lay there in the tall grass knowing your scouts would find me and take me to your camp. I was very surprised when I saw you alive. I recognized your Medicine Man as healer for the Fort from when we traded with him last Spring. When your Medicine Man came to me, I asked if he was your prisoner and he said no. I remembered the General telling me that his boy saw you and the Medicine Man at the big house on the hill. It was then that I knew he is the one that is helping you from getting captured."

White Horse is not happy to hear this and there is only thing that he can do that will save his brother-in-law from dangling from a noose.

"Kill him," White Horse says. Eagle Moon grabs Spotting Bear in a choke hold.

"Wait Chief, wait," Spotted Bear pleads. "I can help you. The General trusts me. I can convince Little Elk to join you and together our band will be more powerful on fighting the soldiers." Spotted Bear eyes plead with the Chief.

White Horse makes direct eye contact with Spotted Bear as he towers over him.

"You betrayed my people and you tried to make me look like a fool."

In a blink White Horse has Spotted Bear by his tunic and pushed up against the rocks. He squeezes Spotted Bear's face forcing Spotted Bear to look at him.

"Oh, you will help me," he growls. "When your body is tossed at the door of the Fort and the General sees it, he will know exactly who he is dealing with."

He then let's go of his grip and Spotted Bear falls to his knees. White Horse looks over at Eagle Moon and nods his head. It is then that the throat of Spotted Bear is sliced. White Horse watches him fall to his death.

Chapter Eleven

The Brave One

First light has hit the Fort gate. The General steps out of his quarters to light a smoke. He is still angry that he was tricked on trusting that Indian. He feels like a fool waiting there for hours at the abandoned Indian camp to ambush the leader of the band of Sioux who has out witted him for months. He thought for sure he had them this time. He is growing really tired of this band and is determined to find them and finish them all off. He inhales some smoke when he hears a soldier come running towards him.

"Sir," the soldier salutes.

"Speak soldier," the General says.

"You are needed at the gate entrance sir."

The General is greeted at the front gate. He looks down on the ground at the lifeless mutilated body of the Indian that he hired. He sees the message that was provided by the arrow sticking out of his back. He knows then that his trap backfired.

"Shit," he says.

Roger has made the ride to the Fort and is on the way to the post office. He has written four letters to Rose within the last two months and he has not received one in return. He is certain that she is just ignoring him and this infuriates him. He sent her a letter today that he is certain would get her attention. He steps across the busy street and onto the walkway leading into the general store.

"Good morning, Doctor Briggs," Corrine greets.

"Good morning," he greets back.

"May I help you with something?" She offers. He glances around at the store.

"Where is Jackson this morning?" he wonders.

"He is resting in bed. His rheumatoid is bothering him something fierce today."

"Oh, well maybe I should go check on him. I bet he is out of that ointment that I gave him."

"He is," she answers.

"I will stop by on my way home and give him some more. He needs to tell me when he is running low, so I can keep him supplied."

"He knows, but he is stubborn," she grins. "I know you did not come here to talk about Jackson's rheumatoid. What can I get for you?"

Roger reaches into his pocket. "I need these supplies," he says. Corrine takes the list and reads it over.

"I can get you the coffee and the sugar, but I am afraid I do not have any corn starch left until the stage comes in this afternoon."

"Oh, that is not a problem. I can come back tomorrow."

"I can bring it to you. It is not a problem. I have to go that way anyway to Grace Tucker's place. She has some things that I need to pick up for the woman's banquet we are having at the church."

"If you are sure it won't be a bother?"

"Not at all."

"Very well then, I thank you."

Corrine goes behind the counter and starts to weigh the sugar.

"The women at the church are missing Rose," she comments.

"So am I."

"Have you heard from her at all?"

Normally Roger does not share personal information with anyone, but he has known Corrine for years and she has always been a dear friend to Rose. She is very close in age to Rose and has never been married. He finds Corrine very attractive and could give his sister a run for her money, but he never thought of her more than just a friend. Corrine has a good heart and is very strong willed. He thinks that is part of the reason as to why she has never married, as it would take a strong man to deal with her. He knows she is not being nosey and is just as concerned about his wife's mental state as he is.

"No, I have written to her several times. She is either ignoring me or she is not getting them."

"Oh, she is getting them," she says, as she puts the scoop full of sugar in the bag.

"You have heard from her?" he asks her perplexed?

"Yesterday," she says. "Her letter is over there on the desk."

Roger glances over at the desk that is at the back of the store. "May I see it?"

"That is why I mentioned it," she smiles.

Roger makes his way to the desk. He sees an envelope addressed to Corrine. He recognizes the curvy handwriting as his wife. He hesitates to grab it.

"I better not," he says.

"Why not?" Corrine wonders.

"Because it is addressed to you. She would be very upset if she knew I read it. Rose is a very private person."

"You are an honorable man Roger," she says. "So, you do not have to feel any guilt on reading it, I will tell you what it says."

"Fair enough."

"Shortly after she arrived there, her mother suffered a heart attack and passed away."

"Oh no," Roger gasps.

"Rose had trouble coping with it and went under a doctor's care for a spell."

"My poor Rose," Roger mumbles. "I need to go see her."

"I would wait a little bit,"

"Why, she is my wife. I need to be there for her."

"She is coming back in a few weeks. She is staying long enough for the reading of the will. Her mother had an attorney to settle the estate. As soon as that is all done, she is returning. She asked me if she could stay with Jackson and I until she figured out what she is going to do. I of course think she needs to be with her husband and I told her that when I wrote her back this morning."

"You mean if she is going to forgive me?" Roger asks.

"I know she loves you. She did ask about you."

Just then Roger remembered the letter that he had just dropped off at the post office. He had to hurry and go get it back before the mail stage got here.

"I have to run."

"Are you alright?" She asks.

"Yes, I have to get the letter back I sent her before the stage picks it up." He reaches for Corrine's hand and gently squeezes it. "Thank you, Corrine. You are a good friend. I will be by later for the supplies," she tells him.

"Don't worry I will bring them with me when I deliver the corn starch." He smiles at her and turns to leave.

Roger is quickly out the door and rushing to the post office.

He was able to intercept the letter before the stage came. He is making his way back to his wagon when he is stopped by a soldier.

"Doctor Briggs," the young soldier says. Roger notices the man standing beside the soldier. He is well groomed in a suit and carrying a briefcase.

"This is Doctor Rupert Collins, your assistant."

Roger extends his hand. "It is a pleasure to meet you. I have been anxiously waiting for your arrival"

"The pleasure is all mine. I have heard nothing but good things about you. The soldier was telling me about your recent loss. My sincere condolences."

"Thank you," Roger says.

"I am on my way to take the Doctor to the clinic," The soldier says.

"I am heading that way myself," Roger states. "I can show him."

"I have my orders sir."

"Very well then," Roger says. "Shall we."

The men begin their short walk to the clinic at the end of the street. Rupert begins the conversation.

"This place is much larger than I was led to believe."

"It has grown in its military strength within the last year," the soldier proudly says.

"I notice you have one guard stationed at the gate. I would think in the middle of Indian country you would be more cautious."

"We only had one minor problem with them getting too close to us, but we quickly taught those savages a lesson by killing their Chief. They will not return."

Roger holds his tongue, as he knows differently.

"I heard," the Doctor begins. "That they marched right into the Fort and annihilated it, killing many of the soldiers."

"I assure you that what you may have read in the paper was all fantasy. As you can tell the Fort is strong as ever."

The men step onto the walkway that leads to the door of the clinic. "Well, they got what they deserved if you ask me," Rupert says.

Roger has heard enough. He looks over at the soldier.

"You have escorted us to the destination, as ordered," he says. "If you would give my regards to the General and his wife for me, I can take it from here."

The soldier tips his hat at Roger and leaves.

"Nice young man," Rupert says.

"Yes," Roger agrees. "If you would follow me inside, please

I will show you around."

Koawa moved us safely to our camp not more than just a few hours further down the plains. We have all settled in and are calling this place home at least for the coming days. White Horse returned late in the evening. He spoke very little about the trip with Spotted Bear, but I know him well and something is bothering him. When I asked if he was alright, he simply said I have everything under control. He asked Koawa to go to Roger's and check on him even though he just left yesterday. This concerns me as to why he would ask him to do that and worried that Roger may be in danger and White Horse just doesn't want to tell me. He has disappeared in the smoke lodge and I have not seen him sense.

Prancing Doe is not eating well. I am starting to get concerned if my milk does not agree with her. I asked Song Bird who is nursing Jumping Badger, if she would mind feeding Prancing Doe for me to see if she handles her milk better. She graciously accepted and fed her this morning.

Roger has returned from the Fort. He showed Rupert around the clinic and made sure he got himself settled in his new place inside the Fort walls. Although he cannot be certain until he sees him in action, he seems to know his medicine and was impressed when he learned that Rupert graduated from Harvard at the top of his class.

He cannot shake the feeling that he knows the Doctor from somewhere. He is terrible with names, but he never forgets a face. Roger at one time would attend seminars at Harvard when he had just started his practice in Willow Creek and would meet many new physicians just starting out. Rubert did say he graduated from Harvard, so he is wondering if that is where he knows him from.

With Max at his feet, he makes the short walk up the hill and sits down in front of his son's grave. He begins to pick the weeds that are starting to cover the tombstone. His mind is heavy in thought over his wife. His heart goes out for her, as she has endured more heartache in the last few months than she has ever in her life. Rose has never been emotionally strong and it does not take much to make her melancholy. Getting word that she is in a doctor's care has worried him, as he fears that she is near or perhaps already has had a nervous breakdown. He can only pray that it is not so severe that she needs to be institutionalized.

His mind then wonders to his son that he held briefly when he removed his lifeless little body from his mother's womb. Despite what Rose said, he has always wanted children and could not wait to hear the pitter patter of little feet running across the floor. He always thought he would make a good father and knew when he met Rose that one day that dream would come true. He wipes a tear from his eyes, as he pulls the last few weeds from the grave. As he was drying them, he sees Max get excited. He quickly turns around and sees Koawa sitting high on his horse. He is uncertain as to how long he has been there.

"Koawa, I didn't hear you ride up." Koawa jumps off his horse and joins Roger on the ground.

"I did not want to disturb you with your son," he says.

"Thank you," Roger says.

Roger does not know Koawa very well, like he does White Horse. Although Koawa has always been kind to him their conversations are always short and to the point. He feels a little embarrassed that this mighty warrior caught him in a weakened state. Koawa looks across at the grave.

"I still remember the day my Running Water died," he says. "The pain was very deep in my heart. I grieved for her for a very long time. It was days before I was able to stop carrying her body around in the blanket. Just having her in my arms made me feel close to her. You are feeling that pain. I can see it in your eyes."

Roger was not going to lose it in front of this mighty warrior. He refused to look like a weak person in front of this proud man.

"It is," Roger agrees. Koawa reaches inside his parfleche that he has draped over his shoulder.

"This is for you," he says. He pulls it out and hands it to him.

It is a pipe. Roger has never been a smoker and finds it to be a very nasty habit. He is pretty certain that Koawa knows he is not a smoker, but not to insult him he graciously accepts the gift.

"Thank you," he says.

"That is a healing pipe," Koawa says. He then reaches into the bag and pulls out a tobacco pouch, handing it to Roger.

"This is very kind of you," he says. "One day we will share a smoke together."

"It is to be used in prayer," Koawa says, "If used correctly it will help you heal."

"I see."

"Giving you the pipe is not the only reason I have come," Koawa says. "White Horse has a message for you."

"What is it?" Roger wonders.

"Your suspicions on Spotted Bear were correct."

"In what way?"

"White Horse knew you were correct with your suspicions. He went with Spotted Bear to see Little Elk, but stopped a few miles before hitting the camp and cornered him. Spotted Bear admitted he was hired by the General to get into our camp and lure White Horse away into a trap. The General was waiting to ambush him at Little Elk's camp. Little Elk had already moved on the day before so White Horse would not have known that he had left."

"Where is Spotted Bear now?" Roger asks.

"Dead, White Horse had little choice. Eagle Moon slit his throat. White Horse had his body tossed at the Fort gate last night so the General would see him and know that his planned failed."

Roger grew concerned. "Is the General suspicious that White Horse is still alive?"

"No," Koawa answers. "He wants to make his presence known, but he is afraid if he does it will give you away so for the moment, he will stay quiet about it. But White Horse wants me to warn you to be very careful on who you trust. He has moved his people to the other side of the river. We will be safe there until the winter. He said the Blue Coat's won't find us there. He wants you to lay low for a while. Give the General no reason to be alerted to you. The scouts and I will keep an eye on you from a distance. You will be safe."

"You and I started out on the wrong foot many years ago," Roger says.

"You have proven to me that you are an honest man," Koawa says, "And very wise. You are not like other White Men."

"I thank you," Roger says, Koawa comes to his feet.

"Please," Roger says, "Let me get you some meat." Koawa holds his hands up to decline. "It is the least I can do, "Roger says, "for giving me this fine gift." Koawa pauses a moment before accepting.

"Great, I will be right back."

Koawa watches Roger as he briskly walks off with Max trailing behind him. He grabs his horse's lead and makes his way down the hill. He stops in front of the creek and squats down. Cupping his hand, he takes a sip of the fresh, clear, cool water. He gazes out into the water and notices the sparkle of the tiny yellow dust that glistens the rocky bottom. He remembers White Horse talking to him about a cave full of shiny rocks that Roger has behind his home. His brother said it is this shiny rock that turns a wise man into a fool. He wonders if this is the shiny rock that his brother is talking about. He is ready to come to his feet when he becomes startled when he hears a gunshot and sees a bullet land in the water next to him. He takes his knife out of its sheave and is quickly on his feet. When he turns around, he is stunned at what he sees for behind that rifle is a White Woman.

"Stop right there Indian or I will shoot again and this time I promise you I will not miss."

Koawa is silent in his moves. He stares over at the woman who is bravely standing her ground. Koawa has looked into the chamber of a rifle before and is not the least bit afraid, especially from a woman who has a terrible aim. He notices behind the rifle a woman with long, wavy hair the color of a sunset. She is slender, but has enough meat on her to emphasize her curves. He finds her courageous, but yet foolish to how unaware she is at how he could easily overpower her and snap that beautiful neck in two. He comes in closer to her in the attempt to grab the rifle out of her hand.

"I said stop!" she yelled, just as she pulled the trigger and went flying back on the ground from the kick of it. The bullet grazes Koawa in the arm.

"Corrine!" Roger yells. He runs up and puts himself in front of Koawa. "Stop this nonsense," he yells. "This man is a friend."

Corrine is covered with prairie dust and has a few twigs coming out of her hair from her fall. The rifle is lying at her feet. Roger quickly takes it out of her reach.

"For Christ sakes woman you could have killed him."

"Well, how was I supposed to know that he was a friend? I saw him at the creek getting water when I rode up. I just assumed he was here to hurt you."

Roger turns to Koawa. It is then that he sees the tear in his tunic and the blood coming from his arm.

"She did hit you," he says surprised, as the Corrine he knows couldn't hit the side of a barn door.

"She just grazed it," Koawa says.

"Come inside and let me clean it up," Roger says.

"No thank you, I am fine."

Koawa cannot take his eyes off the woman that Roger called Corrine. He watches as she dusts herself off and removes the twigs from her hair. He admires her bravery behind all that beauty. He thinks to himself he has never seen such a stunning White Woman. He finds Prairie Dawn beautiful and did not think it was possible there could be another White Woman as beautiful as her. He sees the curves of her legs as she straightens out her dress. The dress is ugly, but she wears it well.

Roger turns to Corrine. "Why are you here?" he asks annoyingly.

"Delivering the supplies you ordered," she answers dusting herself off.

She looks over at the man standing near Roger. She has seen Indians before at the Fort and finds them dirty and filthy, but this man is anything but. She is mesmerized by his majestic appearance. She melts in his dark marble eyes as she embarrassingly removes the twigs hanging in her hair.

"My apologies to you, Mr. Indian," she finally says.

Not to embarrass herself any further she quickly rushes back to her buckboard and pulls herself up. Koawa rubs his arm, as he watches the woman named Corrine turn her carriage around and makes her way to Roger's home.

"Are you sure I cannot clean the wound for you?" Roger asks Koawa.

"No, I am fine. I will have Medicine Moon tend to it when I get back."

"Thank you again for the fine gift. I will use it with great pride."

Roger hands Koawa the slab of meat and watches him ride away, until he is only a speck in the horizon.

Koawa cannot get the woman named Corrine out of his mind. Never has he seen a woman, especially a white one, with so much beauty, and strength. He knows he has to see her again. He must, but how? He will meet up with the scouts shortly and then ride with them the rest of the way home. He has time, he thinks to himself on thinking on how he will meet this woman again.

Chapter Twelve
The Secret

Evening falls across the Great Plains. I am sitting on the pelt that I share with my husband nursing Prancing Doe. She still is not eating much, even with Song Bird. I am starting to get concerned that something may be wrong.

"Come on my sunshine, eat up," I tell her. I can only get her to take a few sucks before she rejects the breast and turns away. I am rocking her in my arms when White Horse walks in. He squats down in front of me.

"It is a beautiful evening my Love. Come join it with me."

"As soon as I get her to nurse I will." I tell him.

White Horse wraps his finger around this daughter's and watches her nurse.

"She has had some restless nights," he says.

"She is not nursing well. I am getting concerned. I don't think she is putting any weight on. I am really worried."

"Has Medicine Moon look at her."

"She did. She is concerned as well."

"I'm sure she is fine darling and you are fretting over nothing

"Maybe," I say, "But I remember the concern Roger had shortly after she was born and that is what has me concerned."

White Horse looked confused. "What concern?" he asks.

"You never mentioned to me that he was concerned about her."

"I didn't say anything, because I myself did not think it would be a concern because I never had an issue with Little Foot and producing milk."

"What is the concern?" he asks.

"That I would not be able to produce enough milk for her, because I am not eating as well as I was with Little Foot."

"I see," he says, "Just to make certain all is well, tomorrow we will go to Roger's. If he says she is alright, then we will not worry any longer."

"You think we are safe?" I question him. "I know you sent Koawa over to check on him. Is my brother in danger?"

"Not anymore. I took care of it," he says. "As for us being safe. Yes, our scouts are between here and your brother's. We will take Koawa with us."

White Horse has never lied to me, but he does keep things from me for my protection or fear. I can't shake the feeling that there is something going on with Roger that is making White Horse concerned enough to have his scouts so far out and near the Fort. He senses my hesitation.

"Relax my Love," he smiles, as he strokes my cheek. "All will be well."

I watch him come to his feet and walk the short distance to the flap. He pauses a moment before stepping out.

"I will be right outside," he says. "Come join me when our child slumbers."

"I will."

An hour nearly passes before I can get Prancing Doe in a comfortable sleep. I am restless with her not eating well and I am grateful that White Horse suggested on going to see my brother tomorrow. Before stepping out into the evening air, I make certain that Prancing Doe is safe and secure in her crib. I find my husband nearby sitting under a tree next to Koawa.

"Our little girl is finally asleep," I tell him. I look over at Koawa and the bandage on his arm.

"White Horse told me, are you alright?"

"Just a scratch," he says. "It looks worse than it is."

I then look out at the huge fire that is glowing in the middle of the camp. This is the time of night that many of our warriors will dance and play games around the fire. Occasionally White Horse will join in the dancing as well as Koawa. But tonight, they are both staying put. "We have many warriors missing tonight," I say.

"Yes," White Horse says. "But rest assured my Love. They are watching us."

White Horse and I both look across the fire when we see a rider coming in. Koawa comes to his feet and excuses himself and disappears in his lodge. We then notice that the rider is Kikimo. We watch him ride up on Spirit Dog and get off.

"Where have you been all day?" I ask him.

"Ma, I am a grown man," he snaps. "I do not have to tell you my coming and goings."

White Horse glares up at his son. "You do not take that tone towards your mother," he barks. "She asked you a question, now you answer it."

"Sorry Ma," he says. "I was out collecting turtle shells and porcupine quill. I knew you were up all night with Prancing Doe and were asleep when I left this morning and I did not want to wake you to tell you."

I grab his hand into mine. "Next time wake me," I tell him.

"Okay Ma I will," he smiles.

"There is food in the kettle inside. Go get something to eat."

"Yes Ma," he grins. I watch him walk away. "And quietly, your sister is asleep." I watch our son walk away to our lodge.

Although I did not give birth to him, I consider Kikimo my blood. He was so little when his biological mother, Flowering Blossom died in a Pawnee raid. He rarely ever speaks her name and remembers very little of her. He has always called me his Ma and never has made me feel like anything less than his mother. I am so proud of him and love him as if he came out of my own womb. There is nothing that I would not do for him. My thoughts are interrupted when I hear my husband's voice from behind me.

"You know he is right," White Horse says.

"About what?"

"He is man."

"Not yet," I argue. "I will keep him a boy for as long as I can."

"He reminds me of me at that age. Carefree, and ready to conquer the world." he says. "You could not tell me that I was not a man. In all sense I was."

White Horse looks at the fire and tosses some twigs into it. I know my husband well and his mind is heavy. I cannot help but wonder if it has something to do with Roger.

"When we return from your brother, I told Kikimo he could go on his vision quest."

"Oh, White Horse he is too young still."

"I went on mine at his age, so did Koawa."

"But things are different know then when you went."

"Only the time has changed darling. He will be fine."

"At least I have Little Foot for a few more years."

"You are an amazing woman my Prairie Dawn. The night is still young. We have not strolled in the moonlight for quite some time. Shall we?"

"I would love to." I faintly grin.

Lord knows how much I love this man and I would follow him anywhere. My life would be lost without him. I come into his waist and arm and arm we begin our walk.

Further down the dark Plains, Blue Thunder is enjoying kneading the well-formed naked bosoms of his Rose Petal, as she moves her hips up and down his shaft. A slumbering Matthew is lying nearby on the other side of the fire.

Blue Thunder has not seen his camp for several days and needs to return soon before he is too missed. He has decided that he will return with his new son, Little Fox and the love of his life, his Rose Petal and make his love for them official by making Rose Petal his bride. He will do this in the next few days. Right now, his thoughts are elsewhere as he is enjoying the love making that she is providing him.

As he nears his climax, he sees her bite her lower lip to keep from calling out with ecstasy and not to awaken Matthew from his sound sleep. Blue Thunder entwines his lips around her and takes a few more thrusts, emptying his white stuff inside her.

Stella has never felt more love in her life than she does right now. Although she has been with numerous men in the pass when she was prostitute, never has she been with a man who was quite endowed as Blue Thunder is. She cannot wait to become his wife and has no fear any longer of what that life may bring her. All she wants now is him and providing him with as many babies as she cans. She is hoping that his seed is already growing inside her as she has been feeling very nauseous the last few days. She comes off from on top of him and lies down beside him. Their lips locked again. She reaches for his shaft and starts stroking it. Before the night passes, they will make love again.

Kikimo enters the lodge and immediately smells the aroma coming from the kettle that is over the fire. He comes over to it taking the ladle from it and scooping up some. He takes a sniff of it. "Rabbit stew," he mumbles. "My favorite." As he takes the bowl to scoop some in, he remembers back to the day that he traded the kettle with this Uncle Leksi. Against his wishes he had to return Spirit Dog to him so he wouldn't be in trouble with the soldier that he stole it from. He remembers how angry he was that he had to return him, but because of his love and honor he has towards his Leksi, Roger, he did the trade. He was only without his pride stead for a few months and was surprised when his Leksi bought Spirit Dog for him last Christmas as a gift. His thoughts are interrupted when he hears movement from his sister's crib. He walks over to it and looks in.

"Hey, my little one," he says to her, as he picks her up he smiles down at her.

"It is late my little one, time to close your eyes." Prancing Doe is wide awake and loving his attention.

"Soon my precious, you will have someone else that will love you as much as me and you will have a playmate in Sleeping Bear. As soon as I become a man, I am going to ask his sister for her hand in marriage. I have everything I need to make the necklace that I will place over her head. This is our secret little one, for your ears only."

"I won't tell anyone," Little Foot says from the entrance.

"Little Foot," Kikimo whines. "Great!" He mumbles, he is not happy that his brother overheard a conversation that was only meant for Prancing Doe's little ears.

"I like Rising Sun. She gives me things." Little Foot says.

"Rising Sun," Kikimo says, as he gently puts his sister back in her crib. "Who said anything about Rising Sun?"

"I heard you say Sleeping Bear."

"I was telling Prancing Doe a story to make her fall asleep and there was a sleeping bear in it."

"Oh," Little Foot says. "Will you tell me the story?"

Kikimo adores his brother, even though at times he annoys him. He would give his life to protect him.

"Go get ready for bed and I will tell you one," he says.

A happy Little Foot rolls out his pelt and tosses his blanket over it. Kikimo begins the same task of making up his own. Kikimo does not make a habit of lying, but he knows his brother has a big mouth and he does not want his news to get out until he is ready. He tells a story to his brother about a spirit who appears as a bear. It is a story that he remembers being told by his grandmother when he was his brother's age. He looks across at Little Foot and sees he has fallen asleep. He smiles to himself.

"You always fall asleep when I get to the good part," he says. He crawls over to his pelt and climbs under the blankets.

"Good night my little brother," he says, before falling asleep himself.

Chapter Thirteen
A Hungry Child

Another afternoon comes across the Prairie land. Roger is in his barn raking his horse's stall. His thoughts are in deep despair and his mind has been wrestling for many weeks. The fighting with the Indians has intensified making it extremely unsafe for anyone to leave very far from the Fort without Military protection. Being friends with the Sioux has benefited Roger and he feels safe out here alone. Although he realizes that the Sioux are not the only tribe out here, they do dominate the land and with White Horse's influence the word has spread to the neighboring tribes on who he is and his friendliness and healing power that he has.

He is not worried about being attacked by Indians as much as he worries about being found out by General Phillips. The General has been trying for weeks to get Roger to move into the Fort where he will be protected and can easily be called on. Roger refuses to do this and when asked why, he lies his way out of it, but he knows the man is not stupid and worries that one day he will trip himself up in his lies.

The General has ordered a meeting with other Army General to discuss the stagecoaches that are being attacked by the Sioux and what they are going to do to bring a stop to them. He has heard that the President of the United States has brought in their top General from the 7th Calvary to lead it. This worries Roger, because this is the same General that was responsible for the loss of hundreds of Cheyenne, when he attacked their camp on the Washita River years back. He has been a menace to the Cheyenne and Arapaho nearly annihilating them. He worries about his sister and the rest of the Lakota if this General leads the expedition.

As a doctor for the United States Army, Roger may be forced to go along on these expeditions to tend to any wounded if a battle occurs. This is something he wants no part in and if necessary, he will resign. He then thinks of what he will do for money if he does. He has a cavern full of gold that if he was to mine it and sell it, he would never have to worry about money for the rest of his life.

However, this causes a problem that could be devasting not only to the Sioux, but to all the other tribes that call this land home if he was to sell it. In order to sell it he would have to stake his claim and then the cavern would no longer be a secret. This in return could cause a frenzy and the land that the Sioux call scared would be ruined by White Man greed.

He thinks back to the time when he first stepped foot into the cavern. It was after his friend Earl the prospector had died from a rattle snake bite and on his death bed, told Roger about it and made him swear that he would never reveal its location. He thinks back to the map that Earl left him with several puzzling clues. Roger has been spending more time than usual in the cavern and believes that the clues are somewhere hidden in there. If only he could figure it out.

His mind then turns to his wife. He is very concerned about her and is hoping to receive word shortly on when she will arrive at Corrine's. His thoughts are interrupted when he hears Max bark. He props the rake up against the barn door and makes his way outside to see what Max is barking at. He is pleasantly surprised to see his sister, White Horse, Koawa and Kikimo, riding up.

"Aho," White Horse greets in his tongue.

"Hello," Roger greets back. "What brings you this distance?" Roger asks.

He takes my horse's lead and with his free hand he helps me down. I remove the papoose from my back. Prancing Doe comes into view.

"She does not want to nurse and will only take a few sips. I know she is still hungry and she is not gaining weight like she should be. I am worried. That is why we came."

"Bring her inside and I will take a look at her." Roger looks over at White Horse. "Take your ponies and put them in my barn. Help yourself to the hay."

White Horse finds it odd with what Roger said, but does not question it and orders Kikimo to take the ponies to the barn and give them some hay. He then follows his wife and daughter inside the house.

"Let me have her," he says, closing the door behind them.

He lays her down on the table beside his medicine bag. He opens his bag and takes out his stethoscope. White Horse and I watch, as he examines our daughter.

"Her stomach is a little descended," he says. "She is hungry."

"I try to feed her, but she is refusing my milk."

"Are you gorging at all?" he asks her.

"Yes," I answer.

"So, you are producing, she just isn't latching on?" he asks.

"She acts like she is hungry. She takes a few sips and spits it out like it is sour or something."

Roger puts his knuckle in her mouth and she sucks on it.

"Her motor skill for sucking is good," he says.

"Then what is wrong with her?" I ask.

Roger walks over to the kitchen cabinet.

"Have you been eating anything spicy or out of the ordinary?"

"I eat what we can find. I did not have this problem with Little Foot."

"When you had Little Foot, we had plenty of buffalo," White Horse says. "Now we are lucky if we can find a herd big enough to feed us."

We watch Roger remove a baby bottle from the cabinet and then open his ice box and pull out a glass bottle of milk. He then takes the bottle and pours some milk into the baby bottle.

"When Rose was pregnant, I bought things that our child would need. She refused to breast feed, so I bought a bunch of infant bottles. If this works, you can have them."

We then watch as he brings a pot out and puts a little water in it. He then places the bottle in the bottom of it to warm up the milk

"You think this will work?" I ask him.

"We will soon find out," he answers. A few minutes pass and Roger removes the bottle from the steaming water. He tests the temperature of the milk on his wrist. He then walks over to Prancing Doe and cradles her in his arms and begins to feed her. The relief on White Horse's and my face brightens up the room when she begins to quickly drink the milk.

"I think she will be fine now," Roger says. He hands me Prancing Doe and the bottle and I finish feeding her.

"You can take Betsy with you. She is a stubborn old goat, but she brings good milk."

"I thank you my brother," White Horse says.

"Anytime," Roger grins. "I have other things that I can give to you that I bought for our child. I don't need them and you do."

White Horse can see the sadness in Roger's eyes. Although he is grateful for the gifts, he wonders if Roger is ready to give them up.

"My brother, your heart is good and I mean no disrespect to you, but I cannot accept them."

"No White Horse really, I want you to have them. Rose and I will have no use for them and seeing them only brings me sadness. I want you to have them."

"Then we accept," I say.

Suddenly, the door burst open and a panicked Kikimo runs in. He stops in front of his father.

"Blue Coats, they are here," he says.

"What!" Roger says. "Damn them." He makes his way to the window and looks out and sure enough he sees a small band of five or six soldiers riding in.

"Quick Carrie, take Kikimo and the baby upstairs and stay still, the floor creeks." I am quickly on my feet and making my way upstairs.

"I will stay with you Father and fight," Kikimo says.

"You will go with your mother and sister. I have Koawa if I need help."

Kikimo was not happy. "But I can help," he argues.

"Don't argue, go!" White Horse barks.

Roger quickly takes the rifle over the fireplace and hands it to White Horse.

"Just in case. I have no idea why they are here."

"Is this why you wanted us to put our ponies in your barn?" he asks.

"Let's just say, I had a hunch."

White Horse is certain that it is more than a hunch and wonders if it has something to do with Spotted Bear. Now was not the time to question his brother-in-law on why he has so much fear in his eyes.

He just makes it to the top of the stairs when he hears Max barking hysterically and a knock on the door.

Chapter Fourteen
A Shattered Healer

R oger opens the door and is taken back when standing before him is Corrine.

"Corrine," Roger says surprised.

He glances behind her and sees half a dozen soldiers sitting on their horses. He notices one of them looking around with his eyes. He is uncertain as to where Koawa is but is certain that he is hiding nearby and most likely watching. Max has pushed his way inside the door and is standing at Roger's feet. Roger only hopes that the dog will behave himself, because for some reason the dog does not like the men in blue.

"They saw me leaving the Fort alone and insisted on escorting me here," she says. "Trust me, I was not thrilled about either."

"Thank you, men," Roger states, "for your fine work on escorting this woman out here. I will see that she makes it back safely."

"No offense Doctor Briggs, but a man of your kind would be of little help to her if you were ambushed by Injuns," a soldier says.

"I told you on the way out here," Corrine snaps, "I will be here for most of the day visiting my dear friend Stella and her precious son."

"Half Breed," a young soldier coughs under his breath. Chuckles from other soldiers are heard.

"That will be enough men," the lead soldier scolds.

"I do apologize for their rudeness," he says. "Men our duty has been fulfilled." The man looks down at Corrine and tips his hat. "It has been a pleasure Miss."

"I thank you," Corrine says. The soldiers turn to leave.

"Doctor Briggs there is a ball tonight to welcome our guest. Your attendance is requested."

"Thank you," Roger says. "But tell the General that I have other obligations."

"That was an order sir."

Before Roger can protest, in uniform formation the soldiers leave. The soldier who was looking around comes up to the spear at the top of the hill. He is perplexed as to why it is here. He says nothing to anyone, but his gut is telling him that something is not right with the Doc. He reaches across and pulls the spear out of the ground and tosses it. He then resumes formation and continues on.

Roger waits until the soldiers are out of sight before calling everyone downstairs. Corrine is speechless when she sees Kikimo and White Horse come down the steps.

"Kikimo go find Koawa," Roger says.

Roger looks over at Corrine, who is frozen solid in fear at the sight of White Horse. Roger touches her shoulder and she blinks.

"It is alright," he tells her. "He won't hurt you, as long as you keep your mouth shut."

Corrine rigorously shakes her head. She then turns her attention to the stairs and sees me coming down.

"I left Prancing Doe asleep on the bed. She drank all of it."

"Corrine this is my sister Carrie and her family," Roger says.

"Hello," I greet.

"Hello," she shyly says.

"What did they want?" White Horse asks.

"They were escorting her out here."

White Horse smirks. "We have them scared."

"And they should be," I chimed in.

Corrine then sees the door open and the boy named Kikimo and the man she shot, walk in. Kikimo walks right past her without even glancing her way. Koawa on the other hand, made his appearance known by walking just inches from her and faintly grins. Corrine's inside flip when she makes eye contact with the handsome warrior. Roger comes up to her.

"What brings you here?" he asks her.

Her eyes are frozen on Koawa.

"Corrine!" Roger repeats. "I know you did not come to see Stella. What brings you out here?"

"Huh, oh," she blushes.

"This came for you." She reaches into her apron pocket and pulls out an envelope.

"I have been filling in at the telegraph office for Emily. As soon as I received it, I wanted to deliver it myself."

Roger opens the envelope and starts reading the telegram.

"I'm sorry Doctor," she says nearly in tears.

I come up to my brother when his face turns white. Whatever is in that telegram is not good. When he finishes reading the telegram, he folds it back up and puts it down on the table. We watch him as he starts gazing out the window. I feel because of the presence of the company in the room that he is trying to remain strong.

"Roger what is wrong?" I ask him.

"Rose's stagecoach was ambushed by Indians. There were no survivors."

I gasped and put my hand on his shoulder. I look across the room at White Horse. His look says it all he is just as surprised as I am.

"Roger I am so sorry," I say. I can tell that Roger is about ready to lose it. We watch him pound the window with his fist. Corrine touches his shoulder.

"General Phillips," she begins "say it happened roughly two days from here. She was in a wagon train that was heading to the Fort when they were ambushed. A family of Mormons caught up to it and went back to the closest town to report it. He is sending a troop there now."

I glance over at White Horse. I know he is thinking the same thing that I am. There is a chance that the attackers were Sioux. I only pray it was not one of ours.

"Leksi," Kikimo says, as he runs over to Roger throwing his arms around him. Roger welcomes the embrace. I can see Roger's eyes starting to weld up. He comes out of Kimiko's embrace. "I need to get some air, excuse me." He then rushes out the door.

I am ready to chase after him, when White Horse stops me.

"Leave him be."

"White Horse he should not be alone," I plead.

"And he will not be. Go check on our child."

White Horse turns to Kikimo. "Go ahead and catch up with our scouts. Tell them to have the women prepare a lodge for Great Healer. He will stay with us until his heart heals."

"Yes Father." White Horse grabs Kimiko's arm as he passes him. "Be watchful of the Blue Coats, keep ears and eyes open."

"I will Father."

White Horse turns to Koawa just before heading out the door. No words need to be spoken, these two can read each other's thoughts, there is no tighter bond than what these brother's share. Koawa just nods his head and White Horse walks out the door.

Koawa glances over at Corrine who is standing by the window. He sees her wipe a tear. She stiffens up when she catches him looking at her. She folds her arms over her chest and steps out of his view.

Koawa can see her strength under all that beauty and her bravery as she tried to hold back her tears in front of him. "Come on Koawa" he tells himself. "Go hold her and let her cry." He watches her step-in front of the window and look out. She is so beautiful he thinks and he wants her so bad. No, he says to himself, this is not the correct time. He leaves her be and steps outside and makes his way to the barn.

Roger is standing near the creek. His heart is shattered. A flood of emotions run through his soul. He is angry with the brutality of his wife's death. He feels guilty for not being there when she needed him the most. His eyes are filled with tears and his body is ready to explode with rage. He is unable to hold it in any longer. He starts kicking at the ground in a frenzy. Dust and rocks started flying around. After several moments of rage, he falls on his knees and weeps.

White Horse has made his way to the creek and watches his brother-in-law come down on his knees. He comes up behind him and quietly stands there until Roger calms down. He remains still for several minutes until he sees Roger remove his glasses and wipe his tears. It was not until he sees him sit down on his behind that he speaks a word.

"Care if I join you?" he asks.

"How long have you been standing there?"

White Horse comes down on the ground beside him.

"Long enough my brother," he says. He hears Roger make a deep sigh and close off all his emotions.

"How can you come here and show compassion to me when it is your people's fault that my Rose is dead."

"My brother, I assure you I am just as angry and baffled as you are."

"Oh, come on White Horse!" Roger barks. "Stop patronizing me. There is nothing that goes on that you are not aware of. Your warriors are responsible for attacking wagon trains for months."

"If you are implying that I ordered this, then you are mistaken. I understand you are angry and wanting someone to blame and I wish I could assure you that it wasn't us, but unfortunately, I cannot. For my warriors are responsible for many attacks on wagon trains. I pray that this is not one of them. I am going to find out who is responsible. This I can assure you."

"For your sake White Horse, it better not be your band."

White Horse does not take kindly to threats, but he understands completely Roger's anger towards him.

"Brother, when Carrie was raped by those soldiers, I had so much hatred for the White Men, especially the ones in blue. She made me realize that not all White Men are evil. This is also true for us."

"I am sorry I was curt with you." Roger says. "I know you and your men would never hurt Rose. Oh, White Horse, what am I going to do without her?"

White Horse puts his hand on Roger's shoulder. "The path will open and you will find the way brother."

"It is going to be so hard without her."

"Yes, it is always difficult to walk a broken path. You are welcome to come back with us and you and Max can stay with us for as long as you need."

"I mean no offense to your kind offer, but I need to stay here and make arrangements for Rose's funeral."

"I understand and no offense taken. Your lodge will be standing awaiting your arrival."

"Thank you and please be careful traveling."

"I am always careful," he says.

"No, I mean be exceptionally more careful."

"What do you know brother that you are not telling me?"

"I have been ordered to attend a ball tonight to honor and welcome General Custer." White Horse stiffens up.

"Long hair is here?" he asks.

"He arrived this morning."

"I do not fear him," White Horse arrogantly says.

"If he finds you he will kill you White Horse and everyone else with no remorse."

"If he finds me," White Horse says.

"He has Indian scouts that know how to track."

"So, do I," White Horse says. "My people did not start this war, your big man in Washington did. He takes what it is not his to take. He brings in his long guns and cannons in the hopes of bringing fear to our eyes and that we will bow down to his commands. He is sadly mistaken, for I bow down to no one. If this General of yours wants a fight, then I will give him one."

"You are aware that he is the one responsible for the devastation to the Cheyenne at Washita?"

"I know who this man is, but he does not know who I am. I will be glad to show him if and when he crosses my path."

Roger is not surprised by White Horse's arrogance. He just hopes that it does not cloud his judgement or underestimate what this General can and will do.

"I will try to find out what I can tonight. May God be with you if your men are responsible for this."

Chapter Fifteen
Long Hair

R oger is dressed in his best and is standing at the side of the ballroom nurturing a glass of brandy. He is watching the packed room mingle amongst themselves and dancing to the ballroom music. He thinks of his wife and how she would be highly enjoying this. She would have been begging him for a waltz across the floor. He was not as graceful as she was and would always be self-conscience about it when all eyes would turn on them. What he wouldn't do right now to have that waltz with his wife.

He snaps out of his trance when he hears loud laughter across the room. He glances over at the bar to see a handful of high ranked men congregating around General Custer. He turns his head away, as the sight of the man disgusts him. He glazes out at the dance floor. He notices Corrine dancing with a young man. She seems to be enjoying his company. He takes a sip of the very dry brandy, as he watches the young doctor, Rupert approaching him.

"A grand sight," Rupert says, "Wouldn't you agree?"

"What do you mean?" Roger asks.

"All this for General Custer."

"Yeah, whoopee," Roger moans.

"Do you have these balls often?"

"No, only when important people arrive or Christmas."

"My first week here and I already get to meet the famous General Custer. This is so exciting."

"Yea," Roger groans. "I can barely control myself."

"I heard about your wife. My sincere condolences."

"Thank you," he says.

"I really ought to meet the General. I was hoping you would introduce me to him."

The last thing Roger wanted was to be anywhere near the arrogant man.

"You have to get used to approaching people of high rank. It is expected of you as a physician. Besides a new song has started and I promised Corrine the next dance."

"Oh, lucky you," Rupert grins. "I have been eyeing her all night. What I wouldn't do to dance with her."

"Honestly, you need to crawl out of your shell," Roger snaps.

He then walks over to where Corrine is sitting and offers her a dance.

"I seriously did not expect you to attend," Corrine says.

"I was not given much of a choice," Roger says. Corrine can see the sadness in Roger's eyes and is furious that he was ordered to attend this ball after getting news that his wife has died.

"I am appalled that you were ordered to come after the news on Rose."

"They don't care," Roger says.

"I would be more than happy to take care of the arrangements for her funeral if it is too much for you," she says.

"I don't understand how this all happened. I just don't understand where I went wrong."

"Roger, you have done nothing wrong. What happened to Rose was an accident."

"I should of went to Boston and got her. I failed her as her husband."

"No, you didn't. You gave Rose so much love and a good life. That women loved you so much. When she lost your son and she knew she couldn't have anymore she felt inadequate as a woman."

"I insisted she go to Boston to heal. I should have fought more. As a physician I could have done more, but I was grieving myself and my mind was not well either."

"Rose always liked the wildflowers in the meadow. I am going to pick some and place them on her grave."

"She would like that." Corrine can see that Roger is starting to get upset, so she changes the subject.

"I don't know about you, but if another man asks me to stroll around the dance floor, I think I will collapse." Roger grins.

"Be warned I think you will be asked by the new doctor."

"Oh lovely," she sighs.

Rupert takes a deep sigh before getting enough nerve to walk over to the bar and introduce himself. General Phillips sees him approaching and to Rupert's relief does the honors for him.

"This fine man is our newest addition, Doctor Rupert Collins. He will be joining you on the trail," General Phillips says.

General Custer places his drink on the bar just long enough to shake Rupert's hand. "I have heard a lot about you," Custer says. "I am delighted that you will be joining us."

"The honor is all mine," Rupert says.

"Yes, most feel that way." he arrogantly says.

"When will we be leaving General?"

General Phillips chuckles. "Anxious, I like that in a person." He smacks Rupert on the back. "You will be going with me the first few times, as General Custer has a few Cheyenne's he needs to deal with first. But rest assured, he will be back in no time. Is that not correct General?"

"Yes. I don't see it taking more than a month to take care of what I need to do."

"Darling," they hear. General Phillips turns his attention to his wife who stops by his side. "You promised me a glide across the floor," she smiles.

"General, if you would excuse me. Must keep the wife happy," he says.

They watch General Phillips and his wife walk onto the dance floor.

"Bartender," Custer says. "Pour the fine doctor a drink."

"Thank you, sir," Rupert smiles.

"So, tell me Doctor Collins, what are your feelings on the filthy savages."

"I think they need to be stopped. They are destroying progress."

"My feelings exactly," The General says.

"I must admit though I was a little baffled when I was asked to join you and not Doctor Briggs. He has much more experience than I do," Rupert says.

"Do not cut yourself short. I understand you are a Harvard graduate."

"I am that."

"That is nothing to be shy about. Only the best graduate from there. Besides it is not experience that I am looking for."

"Oh?" Rupert says confused.

"I need a man who is in favor of the war and understands that a good Indian is a dead Indian."

"I see sir and Doctor Briggs doesn't?"

"Let's just say he is a little too friendly with the enemy."

"I see," Rupert says puzzled.

Rupert is certain he has seen Doctor Briggs somewhere, but just can't seem to remember where. He has been racking his brain on it all day trying to remember.

General Custer glances out at the dance floor to Roger and Corrine. "It is a shame about his wife. I understand she was a good woman."

"I never met her." Rupert says.

"I must not appear rude. I think I will offer my condolences to the doctor for his loss. If you will excuse me, please."

Roger is enjoying his waltz with Corrine.

"You are a very good dancer Doctor Briggs," Corrine smiles.

"Thank you, Rose taught me well," he says. "About what you saw today at my home."

"Your secret is safe with me," she grins. "Rose told me you doctored them and how the one named Koawa rescued her from the Dog Soldiers, so I was not too surprised."

She thinks about the handsome warrior whose eyes make her melt. How she wishes she could see more of him.

"That man I saw coming down the stairs is a Chief?"

"Yes," Roger answers. He is a good man, but I have seen, firsthand what he is capable of doing when he is angered,"

"Do you fear him?" she questions.

"No," Roger smiles. "At one point I did when my sister and him were courting, but over the years I have seen so much in his kindness. I can see why my sister fell in love with him and his people. All of them have welcomed me into their homes and into their lives. They have protected me and nurtured me. They call me their Great Healer. That was a boost to my ego," he chuckles.

"I am surprised Rose went along with that."

"Oh, she did not like it at first. But when she was kidnapped by Dog Soldier's it was White Horse and his warriors that got her out. I owe them my life."

"I am sorry I shot him," she sleeplessly says. Roger faintly chuckles.

"I can assure you, Koawa has had worse happen to him."

So that is the handsome warrior's name she thinks to herself. That is the warrior that risked his life to save Rose. This makes her heart melt even more for this man. How she wishes she could see him again.

"I heard the Chief speak English to you."

"Yes, he does and so does the man you shot," he grins. "So, you can apologize directly to him and he will understand."

Roger chuckles when he sees Corrine blush.

"I assure you he has a gentle soul."

By the flushed look on Corrine's face when mentioning Koawa he wonders if she is sweet on him.

"He is not married." Roger says.

"Who is not married?" she questions.

"Koawa, the man you shot."

Corrine blushes. Roger chuckles. Now he is sure of it.

"When my sister was courting the Chief, they would meet in the meadow when she was picking flowers to display on the pulpit at my father's church." Corrine just looks at him. "The Chief has his scouts watching my place. Koawa will most likely be with them. If you go to the meadow behind my home, there is a good chance you may see him," Roger says. Corrine smiles.

"Thank you. That meadow has the most beautiful flowers," she grins.

"Yes, it does," Roger smirks.

"Don't look now, but General Custer is making his way over here."

Roger is less than thrilled to see. They both pull out of their dance as the General approaches.

"Miss," General Custer says, reaching for Corrine's hand and giving it a kiss. "You are looking lovely this evening."

"Thank you," she says.

"Doctor Briggs, I assume," General Custer greets. Reluctantly, Roger takes his hand and they shake.

"General," he says.

"I want to express my deepest condolences to your wife. Such a tragedy, I want to assure you that I will find the ones responsible for the attack and they will meet my wrath."

"Thank you General." He looks over at Corrine. "Please excuse me. It has been a long day and I am exceptionally exhausted. Good night."

"Good night," the General says. General Custer turns his attention to Corrine. "Shall we take a turn around the floor?" He says.

Chapter Sixteen

Sunflower

Another day is on the prairie. White Horse left with Koawa and a team of warriors this morning to scout. They are near the meadow behind Great Healer's place allowing their horses to graze. He is very concerned about his brother-in-law. Spotted Bear's confession before he was killed is heavy on his mind. He wishes Roger would have come back with him when his wife died so he can keep him protected, as he fears Roger is in danger.

He ordered a few of his scouts to stay close to his homestead and showed them the meadow entrance to the gold cavern in the event they needed to quickly hide. He wishes he could have more scouts here because of the distance to the Fort but will not jeopardize his own camps safety to do it. White Horse does not routinely scout, but because of the situation of fearing Roger is in danger he is doing it.

The meadow is secluded and if it wasn't for Roger showing him the cavern, he would not have even known that it was here. This is good he thinks because it will allow his men to keep an eye on Roger from a safe distance.

Koawa is sitting on his horse allowing it to graze. His thoughts are on the woman that Roger calls Corrine. As much as he fights it, he cannot get her off his mind. He must see her again. How he wants to look into her beautiful eyes and watch her lips move when she speaks. He wants to touch her, caress her cheek and twill his fingers through her beautiful wavy hair. He is surprising himself that he would fall for a White Woman, who next to Prairie Dawn, he finds very dull to look at. But there is something about this woman that makes her different, something he wants to figure out. His thoughts are interrupted when he hears his brother and Chief call his name.

"Where did you go?" White Horse grins.

"I was just thinking about Great Healer," he lies.

"Yes, I have been thinking the same."

"I worry for him brother," Koawa says.

"Me as well, that is why his place is being watched."

"What Spotted Bear said has you disturbed," Koawa says.

"Very much so. I fear the General may be onto Roger. Roger is quick at covering his tracks, but right now his mind is not in the right place. But that is not all that is concerning me," White Horse says.

"What else is there," Koawa asks.

"The attack that killed his wife." White Horse answers.

"What about it?"

"I think it was one of us," he answers.

"I have asked our scouts and I am told no. They were not there."

"I don't think it was our scouts," White Horse answers.

"Then who?" Koawa wonders.

White Horse looks over at Eagle Moon.

"Oh, come on White Horse," Koawa says. "Eagle Moon knows Great Healer's wife. He would never hurt her."

"Not intentionally," White Horse agrees.

"What makes you think it is him?" Koawa asks.

"Grey Wolf went to the sight of the attack. Rose's body had already been picked up by the soldiers, but the remains of the attack were still there. Grey Wolf found an arrow with very distinguished markings that looked familiar to him. When he returned home that evening, he found the exact arrow in his lodge. It was Eagle Moon's. Grey Wolf said he approached Eagle Moon about it and Eagle Moon became very defensive."

"What are you going to do?"

"I am not sure. If Great Healer figures it out, I am going to have a lot of explaining to do."

"Roger is a good man. He will understand that it was an error. They saw the coach and they attacked. They don't know who is on it."

"Oh, brother you didn't see Roger when he heard it was a Sioux attack. He was furious with me. He thought I ordered the attack. He warned me that if he finds out that it was my band responsible that he was making sure that they were held accountable."

"Aw brother. Roger would never turn us in."

"No," White Horse says. "I don't think he would because of Carrie, but I do think he would Eagle Moon."

Koawa disagrees. "No, not the Roger I know."

"Oh, I think he would. He is out for blood."

Before anymore can be said, the conversation is stopped when a young warrior rides up and stops in front of his Chief.

"A White Woman is coming into the meadow."

"She see you?"

"No," he answers. White Horse looks up at Koawa.

"Just watch her, see where she goes."

"Right," Koawa says.

Corrine finds the meadow behind Roger's home. She knew exactly where the secluded meadow was from Rose. They would go there frequently and pick flowers for her table when she would come for a visit. She quickly locates the purple flowers that her friend liked and begins picking them.

Koawa sees the horse grazing in the field and a woman nearby picking flowers. He slides off his horse and crouches down in the tall grass to get a better look. He crawls the few feet to the back of the woman. He watches for a few seconds. He hears her humming a tune to herself, as one by one she picks the purple flowers and puts them in her basket. Wait, he tells himself. It can't be. He crawls on his stomach to get in closer. He watches the woman stand up. It then became perfectly clear. His heart skips a beat, as standing before him is the woman he has not been able to stop thinking of. "This has to be fate," he smiles to himself. He does not want to scare her and run her off, so he crawls back to him horse and comes out of the tall grass to jump on its back. He takes a deep breath. "Come on Koawa," he tells himself. "Don't blow it." He then begins the leisurely walk across the meadow to the beautiful woman. He stops his horse just inches from her and gets off. It is then that she sees him. At first, she seemed alarmed. A little frightened by his sudden appearance. Koawa grins.

"Lovely day to pick flowers," he huskily says.

Corrine is flabbergasted. Roger was correct. She cannot believe that the man named Koawa is standing right in front of her. The man she cannot stop thinking of. She watches him step into the tall grass and stop in front of her. He is surely the most magnificent man she has ever laid her eyes on.

"Yes, it is," she finally says.

"Sorry if I startled you," Koawa says.

"I am sorry I shot you," she blurts out. She watches him smile. He is gorgeous, she thinks.

"You are a very brave woman," Koawa says. "To stand up to a warrior like myself."

"Well," she blushes. Koawa grins. She is so beautiful and he wants her so badly, but he knows in order to do that he has to put his charm on and not have her fear him.

"Do you come here often?" he asks.

"Rose liked it here. Her and I would come here and pick wildflowers that she would put on her table."

Koawa removes a flower from the basket and places it in her hair. "Is that why you are here now?" he asks. "To put them on your table."

"No," she answers. "I am here to put them on her grave."

"Rose was a good woman. She will be missed."

"You are Koawa correct?" she asks.

"Yes," he answers.

"Rose told me of the warrior who rescued her from Dog Soldier's and all you did. You are so brave."

Koawa grins. His groins are on fire as he looks into the eyes of the most beautiful woman he has ever seen. He controls himself to not scoop her up in his arms and kiss those voluptuous lips.

"Why are you here?" she questions.

"Our Chief has us nearby to keep an eye on Great Healer."

"Why? Is he in danger?" she questions.

Koawa gently strokes a strand of hair that is flowing free from her bonnet.

"Not with us around," he answers her. He takes her basket from her hand placing it in the prairie grass. He then takes her hand into his. "Come, let's sit down and talk," he says.

He leads her to a place in the grass and together they sit down. He looks into her beautiful eyes. He watches her remove her bonnet, allowing it to rest on the back of her shoulders. He cannot help but stroke a curl that is blowing free.

"You live at the Fort?" he asks her.

"Yes, I do."

"Alone?"

"With my brother," she answers,

"Where are your parents?" he asks

"My father was a soldier for the Army. He died a few years back. My mother died from fever when I was twelve. Her and I were very close."

He can see the pain in her eyes as she remembers back. He catches a lone tear on her cheek that has fallen.

"That must have been very hard on you both," Koawa says.

"It was."

He watches her close in her tears. Such a strong woman he thinks to himself, but still so delicate. It is taking Koawa everything he has on controlling himself to not plant a kiss on those full lips of hers.

"What about yourself?" she asks.

"I have lost my parents as well. My father who was a Chief, was killed when Pawnee attacked our camp. Both my brother and I were not there when it happened or we too most likely would have been killed."

"The Chief is your brother?" she asks.

"Yes," he is." Corrine is impressed. If his brother is Chief, then he is up there in rank within his tribe.

"Are you married?" she asks, praying that the answer is no.

"No," he says. "I was. She died in Great Healer's sister's' arms when our camp was attacked by soldiers a few years back."

"Oh my, I am so sorry."

Koawa leans forward to hold her hand. He lifts it to his lips and kisses it, for now that is the closest he will get.

"I grieved heavily for her loss for many years, but I grieve no more." Corrine blushes.

Koawa will remain in the meadow for hours just talking to the woman who he calls Sunflower. He knows that the time to say goodbye to her is here, as he is sure White Horse is wondering where he is. He takes her hand and walks her back to her horse. "Stay on the main road," he tells her. "You will be safe."

He watches her ride off, before getting on his own horse and riding back to White Horse. He enters the meadow by the cavern just before the sun reaches its highest.

"I was about ready to send a search party out for you," White Horse says. "Great Healer has had company."

Chapter Seventeen
The Clue

The morning sun peaks its head over the horizon. Roger had a very restless night and has been up for hours. He has just finished his last cup of coffee and will soon be going to the Fort to meet the soldiers who are bringing in the corpse of his wife. He is finding it very hard not to be bitter towards the war party that is responsible. His taste for revenge is bittersweet. He is aware that he is living on land that the Sioux call home and that White Horse is not the only band around. But how can he be certain that the war party that attacked Rose's stagecoach was not from White Horse's band? What will he do if he finds out it was.

Roger is saddling his horse for the ride into town. He is allowing him to graze on the hay that he tossed him, as he prepares him for the journey. His mind is heavy with the conversation he had with an unexpected visit from Doctor Collins yesterday. He remembers now where he has seen him. He was the doctor who replaced him in Willow Creek.

He came last night to drop off some files. Why he couldn't give them to him today when he was there, he finds odd. He remembers the conversation that he had with Koawa warning him to trust no one. He is worried this doctor may know more than what he is leading onto. He also hasn't seen Stella or Matthew for several days.

He is certain that they are with Blue Thunder. He wishes he knew exactly where they were, as Stella would want to know about Rose. He reaches for the halter and rope that are looped over a nail in the stall and grabs his horse's head to put the halter on.

"I am sorry boy to interrupt your breakfast," he tells him. "But we must be on our way." He looks down at Max, who is gnawing on a pork rind.

"Time to go into the stall buddy," he says.

He picks up the bone and tosses it into the nearby stall. When Max runs after it he closes the stall behind him.

He then leads his horse out of the barn and puts the bridle on that is draped over his shoulder. With his horse ready to leave, Roger pulls himself up on the saddle and loops his medical bag over the horn. He then begins the short ride to the Fort.

Somewhere in the hills under a cluster of trees overlooking the prairie below, Blue Thunder has returned to Stella and Matthew with a morning kill. He slides off his pony and rubs the top of his son's head, as he passes by him to go to his Rose Petal.

Stella is tending to the fire when she sees Blue Thunder return. She watches him toss the kill on the ground beside her. He kneels down next to her and gently caresses her cheek. She smiles across at him remembering the heated lovemaking that occurred only a few hours ago. He gently kisses her forehead, before removing his knife from his sheave and beginning the task of skinning their morning meal. His attention is drawn away from her, when he hears Little Fox, Matthew, call out to him and point out into the horizon.

Blue Thunder met up with the scouts this morning when he was out hunting and is aware that Long Hair is in the territory. He is going to be taking his son and Rose Petal back home today where he knows they will be safe. He will then join the rest of the scouts in the search for the notorious General.

He is quick to his feet and hastens his way over to his son, fearing that perhaps it is Long Hair that he sees. Relief sets in when he notices that it is a lone rider approaching. He stands there patiently waiting and when the rider is only a few yards away, he sees that is the Chief's eldest son.

"Father sent me to make certain that you are aware that Long Hair is here," Kikimo says.

"You can tell the Chief that I am aware of this and I will be joining the scouts in their search, just as soon as I get my family back home where I know they will be safe from the long guns."

"I would like to come with you when you take them home. I would like to see how Leski is doing. Are you aware that his wife was killed?"

"Yes, I was told this as well. Rose Petal has not been told yet. Her heart will be saddened by this. Great Healer's wife was a good woman."

"Yes, she was. Last I saw Leski he did not look good. I need to make certain that he is alright."

"I will give word to your uncle that you are thinking of him."

"Please Blue Thunder," Kikimo pleads. "I want to go with you."

"I am not going to be responsible for the Chief's son in the event I meet up with Long Hair."

"He doesn't scare me," Kikimo boasts. Blue Thunder just looks up at him. He knows the Chief's son talks big.

"You are a little man with a big ego," he says.

"If we do meet up with him, you may need an extra set of hands," Kikimo says.

"You make good argument," Blue Thunder says. "But I will not be staying long. I am only dropping them off and then I will be joining our scouts."

"I am joining then as well and we can go together after we drop them off and I see my Leski."

"Does your mother know that you wanting to do this?"

Kikimo just rolls his eyes. He is a man now, a warrior, and a warrior does not need the permission of his mother to leave the camp. Blue Thunder knows Kikimo very well. He is just like his father was at that age. He has an ego that is too big for his tunic.

"Until you return from your vision quest and find your name you are not a man and therefore, I will go by myself." Blue Thunder says.

"But father is letting me go on my quest as soon as it is safe and he is allowing me to go with my Uncle Koawa as he scouts," Kikimo argues.

"Then you can go with your uncle," Blue Thunder says. "He can be responsible for you."

Kikimo is not happy, but says no more as he knows it would be pointless.

Further down the plains. Upon entering the Fort, Roger sees that the soldiers have returned with the victims of the attack. He makes his way to the wagons stopping just shy of them and getting off his horse. He loops the reins around the hitching post next to the trough. The boisterous crowd that he heard as he was riding in has silenced and all eyes are on him. He feels a hand on his shoulder from an onlooker, as he pushes his way through. He stops at the first wagon and raises the blanket that is over one of the corpses. It is not his wife, but he can tell by the condition of the body that the attack was vicious.

"Doctor," he hears the Sheriff say. "I do not think you should see this." Roger places the blanket back over the first victim.

"Where is she?" he asks.

"Please let Doctor Collins do this."

"Where is she?" he sternly asks.

The Sheriff knew there was no talking Doctor Briggs out of it. And who could blame him, if it was his wife among the deceased, he too would want to see her.

"She is in that wagon," he says.

Roger is quick at making his way over to his wife. Approaching the wagon, he notices three bodies lying there. All covered with blankets. There is a soldier standing in the rear of the wagon. He motions to him as to which blanket she is under. Roger briefly hesitates before lifting the blanket off her head. He takes one look at her and immediate rage fills his soul, as he comes to terms with how brutal she died. Not only was she pierced through her heart with an arrow, but her throat had been slashed, nearly decapitating her. He pauses a moment and briefly looks away to compose himself.

"I want her placed in a casket and taken to the church," he finally says.

"Absolutely," The Sheriff says. "I will make certain that she is handled with care."

"I appreciate it." Roger mumbles.

"If there is anything that I can do for you, please do not hesitate to let me know."

"You can find the son of bitches who did this to her," he growls.

"We are doing what we can. Both General Phillips and Custer are out there right now searching for them. I must admit though this one has us baffled."

"What do you mean?"

"Usually, the arrows will tell you which tribe. We are fairly certain that it is Sioux, but the arrow that was found in your wife was different. Unlike any that we have ever seen."

"Different as in how?"

"Come inside and I will show you."

Before stepping into the Sherriff's office Roger looks back at the wagon where his wife lays. He watches for a few moments as two soldiers lift her body onto a stretcher and carry her away.

The Sheriff opens his desk drawer and pulls out an arrow. He hands it to Roger.

"The make of it is defiantly Sioux," the Sheriff begins. "But that feather at the end I believe is an eagle. The eagle is considered the strongest and the bravest bird to the Sioux. Whatever warrior made that must be very high in the tribe, maybe even a Chief."

Roger's ears perked up when the Sheriff mentioned Chief.

"Can I have this?" Roger asks.

"Sure."

"Thank you."

Roger fixes his attention to the arrow. He does not know the difference from one arrow to another. They all look the same to him. This one is no different from the other ones that he has seen, except for the lone eagle feather that is at the end of it. He does not remember seeing this sort of arrow in White Horse's lodge, but then again, he can count on one hand on how many times he has been in there and every time he was, he really wasn't paying much attention. His thoughts are interrupted when the Sheriff reaches across the desk and places his hand on Roger's shoulder.

"My deepest condolences to you. My wife wanted me to express to you how much she adored your wife and if there is anything that we can do for you, please do not hesitate to ask me."

"Just find the ones who killed her and bring them back here alive. I want to see him dandle from the noose."

"We will find them," assures the Sheriff. "Our Indian scouts will sniff them out. I promise you justice will be served."

The high afternoon sun scorches across the Plains. Blue Thunder has returned his family back to Great Healer's place where they will be safe. He will join the other scouts in the search for Long Hair and fight in whatever battle they may come across. He gives his Rose Petal a kiss on her forehead. She was told this morning about what had happened to Great Healer's wife to best of his ability, considering the language barrier that they still have. She was very upset and he consoled her as she wept. He notices that she is still not feeling well and caught her gushing from her mouth early this morning. He wonders if the condition that she has been living in has worn her out. She is not used to his way of life and it does take a bit to get used to. He also thinks it could be because his seed has been planted in her and she is with child.

Although he will miss their daily lovemaking before the start and end of their day, he feels her being back to her normal life will allow her to rest. He rubs the top of his son's head as he says his goodbyes. He then gives his Rose Petal a quick kiss on her cheek and jumps on his horse. He waits to leave until he sees them both walk inside and close the door behind them. Knowing that his family is safe he turns his horse around and gallops away.

Chapter Eighteen
My Sweet Rose

Darkness blankets the great land. Roger is sitting in the chair next to the fireplace. His mind is heavy in thought with anger at the brutality of his wife's death. He concentrates on the arrow and its unique markings. He tries to remember if he has ever seen one in White Horse's quiver case before. He cannot imagine White Horse or any of his warriors wanting to hurt Rose, unless they were unaware that it was her. He is convinced that White Horse would have authorized the attacks on the stagecoach, but why would he allow Rose to be killed? Is it possible that White Horse really is unaware of who attacked it? He finds that hard to believe as nothing passes that man when it comes to his warriors.

Tomorrow his Rose will be laid to rest. It is going to be a very short service and anyone in the town is welcome to attend. But as soon as he can get away, he is going to White Horse's camp to look around. His thoughts are interrupted when he hears Matthew coming down the stairs. Roger welcomes him into a quick embrace.

"What are you doing up so late?" he asks him.

"I tried to wake Mama for some milk, but she not moving."

"I will get it for you," he says.

Roger makes his way over to the cupboard pulling out a cup and filling it with the milk in the pitcher. He hands it to Matthew and watches him drink. Matthew finishes it and hands the cup back to Roger.

"Alright now," he tells the boy. "Off to bed." Roger makes his way back to his chair just as Matthew begins to climb the stairs. He glances over at the arrow sitting on the table.

"Matthew," he says. "Hold up."

"Matthew stops. Roger picks up the arrow and meets Matthew at the bottom of the stairs.

"Your father has taken you hunting? Hasn't he?"

"Yes."

"Does his arrows look like this?" Matthew looks at the arrow.

"No," he answers.

"Are you sure?" Roger asks again.

"Yes," he answers.

"Well come here and get a better look where the light is better." Roger grabs Matthew's hand and hurries him down the stairs in front of the light.

"No," Matthew says again.

"You sure about this. You have never seen this kind?"

"I'm sure. Can I go to bed now?"

"Yes, you may go," Roger sighs.

Roger watches as Matthew disappears up to the loft. "I will find the owner to this arrow." He says out loud. "If it takes me the rest of my life."

Rose was laid to rest in the town cemetery on a hill under a big Spruce tree. Reverend Abrams read a scripture from the Old Testament and Amazing Grace was sung. Corrine was by his side, as was Stella and Matthew. Roger was in a daze and didn't seem to notice or hear anything that was around him. His mind was only on his Rose. His thoughts are filled with memories of his beautiful wife that he married nearly five years ago. How he wishes they had more time together, for there was still so much that he wanted to do with her. His heart is heavy, but he remains strong as the funeral comes to an end. The congregation is quiet as they all watch him drop a fistful of soil on her grave. His head is lowered in grief as one by one each congregation member tosses some dirt on her grave as they pass by. As the people start to leave, he thanks everyone for coming and embraces all their condolences. After the crowd has dispersed, Roger is left alone with his Rose. He comes down on one knee in front of the partially buried grave.

"I promise you Love, if it takes my last breath, I will find out who did this and I will see them hung."

Afternoon sun has hit the Lakota camp, White Horse has taken Kikimo out into the nearby wilderness to prepare him for his upcoming Vision Quest. They have been here since before dawn. White Horse feels that his son is ready and has prepared him the best that he can. The rest is up to Kikimo. They are starting their leisurely walk back to camp. White Horse wants to make sure that Kikimo has no questions and is confident that he will receive a vision.

"Son," he says. "Do you have any questions that I may answer for you before I let you leave on your quest?"

"Well, there is one," he said.

"I suggest you ask me son, because once you are out there you are on your own. Only the Great Spirit will be able to help you."

"My name I know will be no more," Kikimo says.

"If you receive your vision this is true," White Horse answers.

"Well Ma is really partial to my name. What if I get a name that she doesn't like?"

"Son, your mother understands how our culture works. She will support whatever name the Spirits provide you."

"Did you see get your vision the first time you went on your quest?"

"Son everyone is different. What may come to me may not come to you. That is what makes your name unique. It is what makes you, you."

Kikimo was absorbing in everything that his father has taught him and he can only hope that the Great Spirits will answer him and give him a name as proud as his fathers.

"Is there anything else that you are not clear on?" White Horse asks him. Kikimo thinks for a moment.

"Yeah, have you ever been in love?" White Horse was a little taken back by the question, as it was not a question that he was expecting.

"What does that have to do with you going on your vision quest?" he asks.

"It doesn't," he answers, "but I want to know."

"Yes, son I have," he answers, "and I still am."

'How did you know Ma was the right one?"

"Your mother, she trapped me quickly. She was different."

"Because she is white?" Kikimo asks.

"I don't mean her skin color son. When I first saw her, she lit up the Prairie with her beauty. I knew very quickly she was the one I was going to marry."

"What does love feel like?"

"I can only tell you how it makes me feel. When I see your mother, my soul becomes hers. My heart beats only for her."

"Do you still feel that way after all these years?" he wonders.

"Absolutely," he answers. "My love for your mother only gets deeper as the years pass."

"Does it make you say stupid stuff?" White Horse chuckles.

"I sense my son has found a young lady that makes his mind do foolish things."

"Does it ever," he says.

"Well, my son if you are anything like your old man, you will have many that will make you do foolish things."

White Horse was not surprised that Kikimo was smitten with a young lady in his band, as he has seen many of them eye him and giggle when he walks by. He thinks very little that his son is falling in love with one of them and once he becomes a man he will forget about the young woman, as he will find better things to pass his time.

They climb the last hill overlooking the camp. Kikimo spots Rising Sun at the creek. As usual his father ignores her and walks right pass her without even a glance, but Kikimo immediately feels those butterflies turning in his stomach. His knees weakened for her. All he does day in, and day out, is think of her. It must be love he thinks to himself, as no other woman makes him talk foolishness or feel weak at the knees. He has vowed that after his vision quest, he is going to ask her to marry him. Until then he will keep his feelings about her to himself. As he passes by the creek and into the camp, they exchange a look that only each other understands.

Darkness has hit the land and Roger is sitting by the fire

thinking of his Rose. He is not sure as to what he is going to do with his life now, as Rose was his everything and he only worked as hard as he did so he could give her a good life. He has nothing now. Nothing he feels is keeping him here. His thoughts are interrupted when Matthew touches his shoulder.

"Mama won't wake," he says. Roger knew that Stella was a heavy sleeper.

"What do you mean won't wake?" he asks him.

"Mama been gushing at the mouth all day, I tried to wake her for milk, but she is cold."

Roger is quick to his feet. He was suspicious this morning before the funeral that she may not be feeling well, as he saw her rush to the outhouse twice and then again when they were at the Fort. She looked weak at the funeral and unwell, but he failed to ask her because his thoughts were on his Rose. He grabs the lantern on the table and rushes upstairs to check on her. He gets to her bed that she shares with Matthew and puts the lantern close to her face. He gasps, "Oh my God."

Chapter Nineteen
The Trustworthy Friend

Roger has Matthew sitting in the saddle in front of him with Max running alongside them. He is nearly at the Lakota camp. He saw some soldiers riding East, that he was able to avoid. Although he has every right to be riding the way he is, he is not in the mood to explain where he is going and why he has Matthew. He despises the men in Blue for the grief that they are imposing on not just the Sioux, but the all the Plain Indians. He has made it his mission that he will do whatever he can to protect them. That is why he will continue working for the Army. He comes around a bend in the Prairie and immediately sees White Horse's scouts perched on top of a hill looking down at him. He has been at the camp enough that all the scouts know him and he does not fear them. The leader of the scouts, known as Two Feathers, raises his staff at him as if to say hello. Roger waves back, before finishing his ride to the camp a little over three miles away.

The afternoon sun hits the Lakota camp. Medicine Moon and I are at the river dangling our feet in the cool water as we are rinsing the berries that we picked this morning. Morning Dove is sitting on the bank next to a sleeping Prancing Doe, who is in her papoose drying the berries off as we put them in the basket after we clean them. My mind has been on my brother all day as I know yesterday, he buried his Rose. I would have done anything to have been there by his side, but with Custer and his Calvary in our territory it is just not safe for me to leave. I am glad he had Stella there to give him some sort of comfort.

White Horse has been gone since sunup with Koawa and Blue Thunder and we see them ride up just as we put the last of the berries in the basket. I watch him hand his horse's lead over to Little Foot and then disappear in Koawa's lodge with Blue Thunder. With our task of cleaning the berries complete, I grab Prancing Doe in her papoose and head back to our lodge to feed her.

Betsy the goat has been a best friend to Little Foot and he walks her around like she is a horse. He enjoys milking her and has even been caught stealing some of the milk for himself. Prancing Doe is putting on some weight and is drinking an eight ounce bottle every four hours and is sleeping through the night. Any fear I had of her not thriving has diminished as she appears to be doing well. Morning Dove has been a great help to me and spends a great deal of time with me when Koawa is away, which lately has been often. I know him and White Horse have been out scouting more which is concerning, especially because White Horse doesn't usually leave camp for an extended time.

My attention is drawn away from my task when I see a lone rider coming into view, following close behind is his dog. White Horse sees it as well as he steps out of the smokehouse.

"It's Roger," I say out loud. White Horse has joined me by my side and is just as surprised as I am that he is here. We notice he has Matthew with him. Odd I think to myself that Stella is not with him, as I know she is not with Blue Thunder and cannot think of any reason as to why she would leave him in the care of Roger.

We watch as Kikimo greets him. He lifts Matthew off and takes Roger's horse's lead and walks off. I can tell Roger looks tired and very distraught. I know something is wrong. White Horse sensed it too.

"Something is wrong," I tell my husband and before he can respond Roger approaches us. He does not give his usual greeting. I can see the fatigue wedged on his face and the voided look in his eyes. I reached for his hand.

"You look like you need a good sleep." I tell him.

"I need to see Blue Thunder," he says.

"Something the matter my brother?" White Horse asks.

"Stella died in her sleep last night," he says. I gasp. I hear a deep sigh come from White Horse as only yesterday did Blue Thunder tell him that he asked Stella to marry him and that he was certain she was with child. This news is going to devastate him.

"How?" I ask Roger.

"I am not sure. I am completely baffled. She was ill the day of the funeral, but I did not ask her what was wrong. Maybe if I had she would still be here."

"No Roger, don't do this to yourself," I tell him.

"Carrie is right," White Horse says, "You had no way of knowing"

We all see Blue Thunder come out of Koawa's lodge.

"It will be better if I tell him," White Horse says. With that said, we watch him walk up to Blue Thunder and take him into the smoke lodge.

"Matthew?" I say to Roger.

"He was the one who found her unresponsive," Roger says.

"Poor baby," I cry. I need to go to him. "Would you mind watching Prancing Doe for me while I go to him. She is inside in her cradle."

"I would love to."

I find Matthew sitting on a log watching some of the kids play. I come down on the log beside him. His eyes are down. He looks scared and horribly sad.

"You don't want to play with the others?" I ask him. He shakes his head no. I put my arm around him.

"Then you sit right here for as long as you want," I tell him.

"Mama is dead," he cries.

"I know sweetheart, Roger told me."

"I only wanted a glass of milk."

"Excuse me," I say.

"I tried to wake Mama because I wanted a glass of milk. She would not wake up. So, I touched her to get to her wake up and she was cold so I gave her my blanket and then went downstairs so Roger would give me some milk. He came upstairs and said Mama had gone to heaven"

"Oh sweetheart," I console, "You asking for milk is not why your Mama is in heaven."

"You sure?"

"I'm positive," I say as I console.

Over Matthew's shoulder I see my husband and Blue Thunder approaching. Blue Thunder has this vacant look in his eyes. I know he must be devastated. Matthew sees him approaching and is quickly out of my arms and into his. Blue Thunder picks him up to console him. Together with my husband by my side, we watch Blue Thunder walk away with Matthew, Little Fox, in his arms.

Evening is deeply upon us. Many have gone to their lodges for the night. I am in the one that we have set up to Roger making his pelt up that he will sleep on. He hardly ate any dinner and I am very concerned about him. White Horse is as well and has asked Roger to join him in his evening walk around the camp. I will finish with his bedding and then tend to his fire before going back to my own lodge and putting my own children to bed.

White Horse and Roger have made it to the creek bed. It has been a very quiet walk and White Horse can tell that Roger is trying to remain strong, but can see the heartache and can feel his pain. White Horse feels blessed because he has Koawa to always lean on. Roger doesn't have that luxury. So, he is going to make a point on letting Roger know that he is the man that Roger can lean on.

"I can see the darkness you have in your heart," he tells Roger.

"Yes, this is true," Roger says.

"It is always painful to lose the ones that you love."

"I don't know what I am going to do White Horse. A big part of myself died with her."

"Your path is broken brother," White Horse says. "You have lost your way." Roger stops and looks out at the water.

"How do I find my path?"

"You let your spirits guide you," he answers.

"My spirit is dead White Horse. I have nothing anymore. No reason to be alive."

White Horse puts his hand on Roger's shoulder. "My brother, you speak of this because your heart is aching. It has clouded your judgment. You have a family here brother. You always will."

He hears Roger sniff. "Before I knew Stella had died, I was going to come here and sneak around your camp to find the person who matches the quiver that killed my wife."

"You do not need to sneak around my brother, for I know who it was and I have already taken care of it." Roger is surprised that White Horse would admit it.

"Who was it?"

"One of my young overzealous warriors, Eagle Moon."

"Eagle Moon," Roger says. "The boy who is with Medicine Moon?"

"Yes." White Horse answers. Roger, who is usually very calm, is fuming.

"I knew it was you," he yells.

"No brother, "White Horse says. "It was not ordered by me. He was with a group of young warriors who took it upon themselves to raid a stagecoach. When he saw that it was your wife he grew scared, because he knew I would reprimand him for what he did."

"And did you?"

"Yes, right now he is with Grey Wolf somewhere in the hills. He is being taught a lesson."

"I don't know what to say. I want to see him hung for this, but again I don't." Roger faintly chuckles.

"The decision is yours brother. I say that because if it was my wife my revenge and taste for blood would be great. As his Chief, I ask you to understand his error and let him try to make it right, but as your friend I will stand by whatever decision you choose."

Roger turns to look at the water. He knows White Horse is remorseful for what happened and even though he did not order the attack on his wife he is taking some sort of responsibility. He knows White Horse is a good and honest man. He would never allow any harm to him or anyone that he loved. As much as he wants to see Eagle Moon hung for Rose's death, he knows Rose would not approve.

"Rose loved the water," he says. "She wanted a home next to the water. She wanted to see the birds fly across the mountains and dip their beaks into the water to get a drink. She loved birds about as much as she loved water."

White Horse just listens on as Roger speaks from his heart.

"Rose was very fond of Koawa and you," he says. "She worried about you all so much. You were her family. Rose would not want any harm to come to anyone of you. Eagle Moon's life will be spared, but never will I forgive him for what he did. When Rose died, a part of me died with her and I don't think I can ever get that back."

White Horse can hear Roger sniffle and then watch him pull himself together as not to cry in front of this mighty warrior

"When I lost my first wife in that Pawnee attack," White Horse begins, "I cried enough tears to fill that river." He said this so Roger knew it was okay to cry.

"Even the strongest and bravest warrior cries," he said.

Roger couldn't hold it in any longer. White Horse watches him come to his knees and weep. White Horse squats down beside him and places his arm across Roger's shoulders and will remain there consoling him for as long as he is needed.

Chapter Twenty
A Doctor's Ploy

Blue Thunder rests on his elbow as he watches his son, Little Fox sleep. His heart is filled with love for the little boy that he has only known he had fathered a few months ago. He misses his mother; his Rose Petal and his heart is heavy with grief for the only woman that he has ever truly loved. He only wishes he knew how she died. He has promised himself that he will raise Little Fox as a Sioux and make him into a strong and proud warrior like himself.

He will be leaving at first light to perform a ceremony for his Rose Petal to make sure she crosses over. He will leave Little Fox in the care of the other women until his return. He reaches for the blanket that his son kicked off and puts it back over him before attempting to try to get some sleep himself.

I am lying on the pelt in my husband's arms. Little Foot and Prancing Doe are asleep. Kikimo will be out for the night keeping watch of the camp. I curl up next to White Horse.

"Sure, still tonight," I tell him.

"Yes," he agrees, "Was very quiet when Roger and I returned."

"Do you think he is alright?" I ask.

"He has a lot of healing to do, but I think he will be alright."

"I wish I knew what to do for him."

"Just do what you do best," he says. "Love him."

This was something I had no issue with and was very good at.

"When is Kikimo leaving on his quest?" I ask, changing the subject.

"I told him today that he will have to postpone it for at least a few weeks. Roger told me today that he saw some soldiers East of here about half a day. That is closer than I like. That is why I have my scouts out all night and they will remain that way until Long Hair is gone."

"Why can't we just move the camp?" I ask.

"Because right now he doesn't know where we are at and by moving, we are taking a chance of being tracked. Staying here my men can cut the trail and lead them away."

"What about Roger?"

"He told me he is going to go back home. He can't protect us if he doesn't know what they are doing."

I hate the idea that Roger is risking his safety and his life for us. He has always been so careful because of Rose, but now that she is gone I worry he will become bolder."

"You brother is no fool Love. He knows the risk he is taking. I assure you he doesn't wish to be at the end of a rope. I as well, will not allow any harm to him."

"I just…" I begin to say. White Horse is quick at stopping me mid-sentence. He rolls over on top of me.

"Less talking and more loving," he whispers in my ear. "I need my wife." With that said, his advances and lovemaking begin.

Roger lies awake too restless to sleep. He takes out his journal and starts writing down his innermost thoughts. Up until the last few months Roger has never kept a journal. His wife did faithfully and never miss an entry. He dips his pen into the ink and begins.

Dear Diary,

The last few weeks have been such a blur. If it wasn't for my sister and my Lakota family, I am not sure if I would have survived. The Chief and I have become very close and I have seen his tender side. I can understand why my sister married him.

These people have lifted me up and shown me how to become a strong man and have taught me the purpose of my life.

I am very worried about them, as the Army is circling around them. I am doing what all I can to relay what messages I can to them, so they are able to stay one step ahead. My sister is very concerned about this, as if I was to get caught it could be my life. I have grown to love this family and right now they are all I have. I am committed to do whatever I have to do to keep them safe. Tomorrow I will return home where I will continue my devotion to my Lakota family. Until next entry.

Roger.

He blows the paper dry before closing his journal. He places it under his pillow. He then hears Koawa outside the flap.

"Come in my friend," he says. Koawa steps in with a blanket in his hand.

"I have brought you another blanket. The evenings can be quite chilly," he says.

"Thank you. My sister has made my fire high. I should be fine."

Koawa places the blanket down at Roger's feet. He turns to walk away. He wants to ask about Sunflower, but not sure if he should. He hesitates at the flap door.

"Is something on your mind?" Roger asks. Koawa comes back over to him and sits down in front of the fire.

"White Horse told me about Eagle Moon. You are a good man Roger, as I am not sure I would have been so eager to forgive."

"Rose thought very highly of you, all of you, but especially you," Roger begins. "She would not want any harm to come to any of you. I am doing it for her not for me."

"Rose and I started off rough, but I liked her. She was a good woman."

Right now, all Koawa can think of is another good woman who he would love to have on his pelt right now. Roger can sense that there is more on Koawa's mind than Rose. He knows that Corrine was in his meadow picking flowers and is very sweet on him. He wonders if Koawa feels the same. He does not know Koawa like he knows White Horse, but if it wasn't for Koawa saving Rose from the Dog Soldier's last summer, she never would have survived. He owes this man a lot and has a great deal of respect for him.

"May I ask you something that may not be any of my business." Roger says.

"Of course, you can ask me anything," Koawa answers.

"I sent Corrine to the meadow to pick flowers, because I knew she was sweet on you. Did you see her?"

Koawa clears his throat. He had no idea that Roger was the one who sent her there in hopes that he was there and no idea that Sunflower was sweet on him. This brings him great joy to hearing this. Roger can tell by Koawa's demeanor that he hit the nail on the head. "You said I could ask you anything," Roger smiles.

"Yes," Koawa finally admits. "I saw her."

"Well?"

"Well, what?" Roger rolls his eyes.

"Koawa this woman is beautiful and has a heart to match it."

"I know that."

"Do you have any idea how many men danced with her at that ball?"

Koawa was not happy that other men had their arms around his Sunflower, as he only wants it to be his arms that are around her.

"If you don't snatch her up someone will," Roger says.

"Why are you telling me this?" Koawa asks.

"She is perfect for you. I knew that the night of the ball."

"In what way?"

"She has the love for your people, like my Rose had and I have."

"I will admit." Koawa says. "I do want to see her again, but I do not know how I can. She is in the Fort."

"I can help. If Corrine wants to see you again and I am pretty sure she does, I can get her to my house. I do not think the meadow is safe though. I think you should take her to the cavern at least until Custer leaves."

Koawa wants nothing more than this. His body aches to be near her.

"Okay" he says. "I am still watching your place, so I will be in the meadow."

"Good," Roger says. "I will let her know." Koawa comes to his feet.

"Try to get some sleep."

"I will."

Koawa leaves and walks back to his lodge thinking of the woman that he wants as his.

The morning sun is upon us. I am up bright and early with a hungry Prancing Doe. I take her outside so as not to wake Little Foot. White Horse was up awake before me and has gone in solitude for his morning prayer. I am removing the bottle of goat's milk from the kettle and testing the temperature with my wrist when I see Roger step out of his lodge.

"Good morning my brother," I greet him.

"Good morning," he greets back. He is quick at taking my daughter from my arms and the bottle and coming down on the ground in front of his lodge to feed her. I smile as I watch him goo and gaa over her and make silly faces. My heart goes out for him. He not only has lost his wife, but he has also lost his child. Watching how he interacts with Prancing Doe I am certain he would have been an excellent father.

"You are a natural," I tell him.

"It's the doctor in me," he grins. He spots a young Lakota woman staring at him. She shyly grins when Roger catches her eye. "Who is she?" Roger asks. I look over to see who he is looking at. "That is Blue Bird," I answer.

"She is very beautiful," he says.

"She seems to like you," I smile.

I could see Roger starting to blush underneath the rim of his glasses. He has never considered himself a lady's man and I think that Rose was his first and only woman he has ever courted. I catch him glance her way again and smile at her.

"As soon as White Horse returns, I will be making some breakfast, you are welcome to join," I say changing the subject.

"Thank you, Koawa gave me an invitation as well although with his it requires me catching it first."

I smile because Koawa loves to fish and will eat it anytime of the day and nearly any way it is made. Fishing is one thing that sets White Horse and Koawa apart. Although White Horse can and will fish, he would much rather hunt game.

"Mine is already caught and skinned," I smile.

"That will be great. Thank you," he says.

Roger looked horribly tired and although he went to his lodge early, I am not sure as to how much sleep he got. I know Koawa invited him to sit around the big fire in the center of camp, but Roger politely declined. I worry about him going home to the place where there is so many memories and has been so much death. It was almost as Roger has read my mind when I hear him say.

"I must return home today. I have things I need to take care of."

"I wish I could go with you. I do not like you being alone at a time like this."

"I do not imagine I will be alone for very long. Corrine is a dear friend of both Rose, and me, and Stella too. I am certain she will be there at some point." He lied, as he was making a point to talk to Corrine about Koawa.

I look to see Koawa approaching. He greets us in his tongue.

"Have you seen your husband?" he asks me.

"He went to go pray," I answer. "Something wrong?"

He looks down at Roger. "Let's walk," he tells him.

Roger looks perplexed. Koawa wasn't asking Roger to join him, he was telling him. Roger puts the near empty bottle down and hands me Prancing Doe before coming to a stand. I then watch as they walk away to find White Horse. "Something is up," I mumble to myself.

Koawa is certain that he knows where his brother is and he is quick at taking Roger into the trees. Within a few minutes, he finds him sitting under a tree overlooking the camp. White Horse comes to his feet when he sees them. Koawa wasted no time at making Roger aware as to why he has been summoned here.

"I met Grey Wolf this morning," he begins. "Early this morning him and his party tracked Long Hair's men West of the creek." White Horse grew stiff, for West of the creek is very near the camp.

"Okay grab all the warriors and cut the trail. Pack up only what we can carry on horseback. We leave in an hour."

"Let me go ahead White Horse," Roger says. "I can find them and try to slow them down or detour them."

"You think you can?" White Horse asks.

"I can buy you a little time."

Koawa shakes his head no. "It's too dangerous."

"No, I can do it," Roger assures. "I have met Custer and the Doctor I trained is riding with him. They will believe me."

White Horse is liking the idea, but Koawa is not as sure.

"It will give you some time to get ahead of him." Roger says.

"Go," White Horse says. "Do it. When we are safe, I will give you word on where we are."

Roger quickly runs off and back to camp, followed by White Horse and Koawa. By the speed that I see White Horse racing into camp I knew my worst fear was true. We have either been spotted or the soldiers are moving in too close. I hear White Horse yell in his tongue for everyone to quickly pack what can only be carried on horseback and get ready to move. For White Horse to move us in broad daylight the soldiers had to be close. This brought sheer panic to me. I see Roger rush past me. I catch up to him.

"Stay close to me," I tell him.

"I am not going with you. I am going ahead and try to slow the soldier's down," he says

"No Roger," I plead. "It is too dangerous."

"I have to try," he argues.

Fear fills my soul at the idea of Roger coming face to face with our enemy. If there was any slip up, or any part of his story was not believed it could be death of him. White Horse comes up behind. "Come on Love," he says, "We must move fast."

I know there is no talking Roger out of this and we have no time to waste or argue. I give him a hug. "Be careful," I tell him.

"I will," he said.

I rush to gather up all my children including Morning Dove. Poor Little Fox is scared to death and Blue Thunder has already left camp and has no idea what is going on. I only pray he will remain safe as I grab Little Fox and put him on my horse. He is going to ride double with me. Little Foot grabs Betsy and ties her to his pony. The goat is going to slow him down, but if it wasn't that I needed her milk she would be left behind. I see Roger jump on his horse. Koawa pats the horse's rump as I hear him say, "Be careful." I then see Roger take off in a full run.

"Lord be with him," I say under my breath.

The women and older children are rushing around packing up what we can in the time that we have. Lodges are taken down and rolled onto a travois or attached to a horse. My kettle is strapped to my pack horse, as is my personal belonging bag and our blankets. Behind the pack horse is our lodge, Prancing Doe's cradle, and a few of our belongings. I make sure that Morning Dove and Little Foot are mounted and ready to go.

I help a few of the elders get onto any free horse. We are to ride double with any small children. Fortunately, we have enough horses that very few of us are having to walk. I mount my horse with Prancing Doe in her papoose on my back. I tell Little Fox to grab onto the horse and hold on. Medicine Moon comes up on my right. She will ride beside me the entire trip. She is my protector when White Horse or Koawa are not able to be. There is nothing and I mean nothing, will get to me without going through her. She is also heavily armed. I have Little Foot and Morning Dove behind me. Rising Sun, who has Sleeping Bear in front of her is on my left. Minoke is behind her. In less than an hour we are packed up and being led by White Horse to safety.

Roger catches up to Custer and his men. He is surprised at how close they were to the camp. Another few hours on the same path and they would have been found. He slows his horse to a leisurely walk and thinks about his next move. He must slow Custer and his men down or lead them in the other direction to allow time for White Horse and his band to escape. He starts the walk down the small hill coming up in front of the soldiers. They stop in front of him. He spots Custer immediately. He sees Rupert and a few other soldiers that he knows from the Fort.

"Doctor Briggs," Custer says. "What brings you all the way out here?"

"I am on my way home from Fork Creek," he says. "They have no doctor there, so I went to see if anything was needed."

"Your wife just passed, correct?"

"Yes," he answers. "I don't see what that has to do with anything."

"Well, I would think you would be home or at least tending to the ill at the Fort, being that Doctor Collins is with me."

"General Phillips has generously given me time off so I can grieve."

"But yet you go adventure to another town to doctor. Why is that?"

"I told you they have no doctor there. I routinely pay them a visit every few months. My duties at the Fort keep me busy and unable to travel to other towns. I needed to get away from everything and clear my head, so I went there to see if my services were needed."

Roger is not sure if the General is buying his story. He is clearly one of the hardest men to read. He is also one of the most arrogant.

"Tell me Doctor Briggs, in your little adventures have you come across any Indians?"

"Yes, I saw a war party on a hill yesterday by Hanson Mill. I was able to avoid them by dodging into some bushes before they saw me."

General Custer just stared him down. Roger can't stand this man, nor does he trust him, but he needs to keep playing the bluff to allow White Horse time to get away. The General looks at his horse.

"I see no rifle on your horn."

"There is no need to carry one."

"This war party you saw. Where they Sioux?"

"Couldn't tell you," Roger says.

"But you have doctored for them before, right?"

"I doctor to wherever my services are needed."

"So, you have?"

"Yes, I have on a few occasions. Why all these questions?" Roger wonders.

"I am just curious as to why you would ride alone in hostile territory without any protection. Unless you knew you didn't need any?"

"I am foolish on this," Roger states. "I forgot to bring my rifle. That is why I ran and hid when I saw the war party."

Custer turns his attention to the Indian scout he has with him. "Have you ever known anyone to see a Sioux war party on top of a hill and them not seeing you first?"

"No sir I have not," he answers. Custer turns his attention back to Roger.

"I guess it was just your lucky day."

"The Lord is good," Roger smirks.

"Sergeant," Custer says.

"Yes sir," the Sergeant answers.

"Get the exact location from the good Doctor on where he saw that party and then we will turn our men around and go to it. "

"Yes sir," he says as he pulls his horse up next to Roger.

"By Hanson Mill," Roger says. "Just after Fork Creek."

"Hanson Mill?" he says. "You sure?"

"Yes sir. I am sure."

Roger was growing a little uneasy and was relieved when the Sergeant turned his horse around and went into line with the others. He looks over at Custer.

"Good day Doctor," he says.

"Good day General and safe travels for you and your men."

"You as well. I strongly advise you Doctor to go back home and stay near the Fort until we can find the hostiles."

"Yes sir. I will do that."

Roger then turns and walks off. He is not sure if his lie was believed, but at least he was able to buy White Horse some time. The General and his soldiers watch as the Doctor rides off.

"Sir," the Sergeant begins," we were just at Hanson Mill and there are no hostiles there."

"I know," he says.

"Do you still want to turn around sir?"

"No Sergeant. We continue forward to the savages. Bloody Knife has tracked them this far. I know we are close. When we return to the Fort, I will have a little talk with General Phillips about his Doctor. Something isn't right."

Chapter Twenty-One
The Mischievous Doctor

General Custer and his men found the abandoned Lakota Camp. They are looking around for any clues on which direction the savages may have gone. The scouts he has hired have been searching for tracks. They are finding very little and have reported back that the Sioux have cut the trail and they are not certain on which direction they went. The General is furious as they have only missed them by a half day or less. He is growing tired of playing cat and mouse with them and he is certain this is the same Lakota band that lost their Chief last year. He is certain it is just a matter of time, before he finds them and destroys them.

Rupert is looking around and stumbles into one the of the abandoned lodges. He glances around and spots an item he knows well, as he carries one himself. It is a medical bag. He opens the bag and sees it that is heavily stocked with everything one may need in an emergency. He looks at the insignia on the clasp. "R.B." he knows for certain who this bag belongs to. "Roger," he mumbles.

Rupert grows still a minute as, he remembers where he knew Doctor Briggs from. He only met him once briefly when he came to Willow Creek to replace him. Roger had showed him around. He remembers a conversation he had with him when he asked why he was leaving his practice in Willow Creek. Doctor Briggs told him that he was leaving, because he no longer had any family there after his father passed away and his sister got married and moved. It wasn't until after he had left that the real reason came out. He discovered that the small town was being under sieged by renegade Indians and a young Lakota Sioux Chief came in to help them and chase the renegades away and for payment he took a white Woman as his bride. The Doctor's sister.

"What do you have their Doctor?" a soldier says.

Rupert jumps as he thought he was alone. He isn't sure as to what to do. He likes Roger and his heart goes out for him on the loss of his wife. He thinks there must be an explanation, as to how his bag got into a Sioux camp.

He then thinks about how nervous Roger looked when they met up with him on the plains. He knew his story on rendering medical aide to Fork Creek was a lie, because Fork Creek just brought on a new doctor a few months back. If Roger is helping the Indians, he is in a great deal of trouble. He looks up at the soldier.

"Nothing," he says. "I dropped my medical bag when I tripped."

He picked up the bag, covering the gold insignia towards his chest so the soldier couldn't see it. He has decided he will confront the good Doctor and strike a deal with him for his silence.

"Be careful their Doctor. We can't have you injured. Who would tend to my rheumatoid?" he smiles.

"Yes, I will be more careful," he says.

"Men," they hear. They turn their attention to the entrance and salute the General once he steps in.

"We are about to head out, is everything clear in here?"

"Yes sir," the soldier says.

"Very well then, mount up," he orders.

He watches the Doctor and his soldier leave. He glances around the lodge and is ready to walk out when something catches his eye.

He picks up a journal off a pelt. He flips it open and starts to read some of the entries. He smirks. He places the journal in his belt and then makes his way out and mounts up with his men.

Further down the Prairie, we have moved our camp. The one we are at now is very well secluded and tucked between two bluffs. It is very beautiful, but very rocky and hilly. The prairie grass is high, providing us with more seclusion and the river is engorged providing us with plenty of water.

The wildlife here is abundant, except for the buffalo which is becoming more difficult to find. Many predators have come close to camp, so for that reason no child is allowed outside the perimeter after dark by themselves and must have an armed escort with them if they must relieve themselves in the middle of the night. White Horse even insists I follow the same rule.

Betsy, our goat was nearly attacked by a pack of wolves. If it wasn't for Medicine Moon, she would be dead. For her safety she is tied outside of our lodge and is only let free by Little Foot who will lead her to food. I can tell she is not happy by this, but Prancing Doe is not old enough yet to go without the milk that Betsy brings and I am not taking the chance of her being a packs meal.

Our war party and scouts have not located any soldiers, but White Horse is certain they are out there and it is just a matter of time before they or us are spotted. This has put all of us on edge. He has warriors scouting on each bluff overlooking the camp and has stationed his war parties and scouts out by several days. White Horse is doing everything that he can do to keep us all safe. Koawa is still watching Roger place despite the danger that it involves.

Matthew, Little Fox, has finally settled in, and has become Little Foot's best friend. I have made him up a pelt next to Little Foot's where he will sleep until his father returns. There has been no sight of Blue Thunder. White Horse insists that he is fine and just needs time to find us. I can tell he is growing concerned that he has not returned and we can only pray he hasn't run into Custer.

Roger met up with Corrine and she is just as anxious to see Koawa, as he is certain Koawa is to see her. Corrine is planning a visit to him where she can meet up with Koawa. Today Roger is sitting at his table nearly all afternoon studying the map that Earl made that stakes his claim. He is certain that the numbers each represent a step, but to where the starting point is, is what he is trying to figure out. He cannot imagine what more Earl could be hiding, as he is literally sitting on a gold mine. There is so much gold here that if Roger was to mine it, he would be the wealthiest man in the world.

He comes to his feet to pour himself a cup of coffee, when he hears Max scratch on the door and then hears a knock. He assumes it is Corrine. He is surprised when he opens the door and sees Rupert Collins.

"Rupert, what a surprise," he greets.

"Good day Doctor Briggs," he greets back.

"Please you do not need to be so formal with me, as we are colleagues. Please come in."

Rupert steps in as Roger closes the door. In his hand he is holding Roger's medical bag.

"I did not expect you back so soon," Roger says.

"General returned for supplies and some well needed rest. They will be leaving again the day after tomorrow."

"I see. I take it they didn't find the war party I told them about," Roger says playing dumb.

"No, but we did find an abandoned camp. We just missed them."

"Oh, what a shame," Roger smirks.

Roger was keeping calm, but so happy that his loved ones escaped and are still safe.

"Funny thing though," Rupert begins, "looking around that camp I found this."

Rupert hands him his medical bag. With everything going on and the rush to leave the camp, Roger forgot he left it behind.

"I thought I lost that forever. My father gave me this bag. Thank you for bringing it back."

"Why would your medical bag be there?" he asks.

"It was stolen from me a few weeks back when I was stopped by a war party. I was scared for my life. One of the warriors was eyeing the bag, so I gave it to him for my life. That must have been the Band that stole it. "

A believable story Rupert thought with the exception he knew Roger was lying. Roger glances down and notices that Rupert is wearing his gun belt and has his hand over the revolver. Roger suddenly becomes uneasy and glances over at his father's rifle over the fireplace. He turns his body slowly towards it to grab it quickly, if need be, when Rupert's expression turns cold.

"I have been wracking my head for days trying to remember where I have met the Doctor Roger Briggs. Then I remembered. I replaced you in Willow Creek. Shit hole of a town." Rupert grumbles. "You told me that you were leaving Willow Creek because your father died and your sister got married and left town."

"That's correct," Roger says.

"But that isn't the real reason. Is it?" Rupert says.

"I have been doing some checking on you and I wired a friend of mine at the last Fort that you worked at. It seems they have questions for you."

Roger is confused as to why his last place of employment would want to speak to him.

"About a murder of a shop keeper who disappeared. Bones were found at your old homestead buried in a flower bed. The sheriff remembers how nervous you were when he surprised you at your place. You were planting flowers in your flower bed. He thought it odd how callous you were when he asked you if you wanted to join them in the search for him. And how one winter he sees a big fire in the sky from your place. When asked, you said you were burning your trash. But you weren't burning your trash, were you? And the time you had an Indian attire at your home and you told the sheriff that you were sleeping in it."

Roger grows very still and is becoming very nervous.

"You have been helping them. You are the reason those heathens are staying one step ahead. Your medical bag was there, because you left it there when you left in hurry to try to slow down the General.

"What do you want?" Roger asks, holding up his hands.

"Your gold for my silence," he says.

"What gold?" Roger says. "I have no gold." Roger lies.

"It is no secret that the Prospector who once lived here had a claim. You know damn well where it is, and I want it."

Rupert then clicks the revolver and points it at Roger. Upon doing this, Max, seeing the danger to his master growls and then pounces on Rupert knocking him to the ground. The revolver goes flying. Roger is quick at grabbing the gun and calls Max off. He points the gun at Rupert. Rupert is not a big man by any means, but he is fast. He lunges at Roger and both are knocked on the ground. Max is hysterically barking and tearing at Rupert's leg. Rupert kicks at the dog, as he fights with Roger for the gun. Roger wrestles the gun out of Rupert's hand and kicks it away out of his reach. They are now wrestling each other on the ground. Roger is not a fighter, but he is giving it everything he has.

Rupert is on top of him and has his hands around Roger's throat and begins to squeeze the life out of him. Max jumps on Rupert's back. Rupert frees one hand around Roger's neck to push the dog off, but not before he is bitten. Rupert bellows in pain allowing enough time for Roger to break free. Rupert then punches Roger. Roger is fighting back, as Max is tearing at the trousers of Rupert.

Suddenly, Roger sees Corrine out of the corner of his eye jump on the back on Rupert. It was enough to take Rupert off guard and Roger to roll free from his grip. As he is catching his breath, he sees Rupert reaching behind him to pull Corrine off his back. Roger runs for the gun. He cocks it and aims, but because of Corrine is unable to get a clear shot. He races to help Corrine, but not before Rupert has her overpowered and tosses her off him. Corrine hits her head on the table and is in a daze.

Both men reach for the gun. Max the dog, once again has Rupert by his leg pulling at his trousers. A groggy and dazed Corrine spots the rifle over the fireplace. She makes a run for it and grabs it. She cocks it hoping that it is loaded. She then aims and shoots, hitting Rupert in the arm. Corrine is frozen with fear when she sees a very angry Rupert coming after her.

Roger grabs his leg to stop him from attacking her, but is stunned when Rupert backhands him with a hard punch. Corrine lets out a scream when Rupert grabs her. Just then she sees Rupert's eyes go still when a tomahawk slices open his head and he falls dead to the ground. Roger looks at the door to see both Koawa and White Horse.

White Horse is quick at Roger's aide.

"Your timing is impeccable," he tells White Horse.

Koawa reaches down to Rupert, pulling out his tomahawk from his brain. He looks over at a stunned Corrine. He squats down, when he sees that she is bleeding from her head.

"You are hurt," he says.

"I'm alright," she says, as she stares at the handsome warrior. He touches her face ever so gently. "Thank you," she softly says.

Koawa grins into the eyes of his Sunflower. How his inside burn with rage that someone would dare hurt her. He sees how strong she is trying to be, even though he is certain she was terrified. He strokes her cheek.

"I will always protect you," he softly says, "my Sunflower."

How he wants to hold her right now. Let her know that is alright to cry in front of him. How he will wipe all her tears away and always make sure there is a smile on her face. There is nothing he would not do for her.

"Corrine," Roger says rushing over to her.

"I am alright," she says.

"No, you are not," he says. "You hit your head hard. You're bleeding."

"I'm fine, honest," she says.

She begins to come to her feet and gets dizzy from the hitting of her head. Koawa is quick and lifts her up into his arm.

"On the bed," Roger says.

Koawa then walks her into the bedroom and lays her down on the bed, leaving Roger to attend to her injury.

While Roger is tending to Corrine, Koawa and White Horse drag Rupert's body outside and toss it in the creek. Koawa tosses a few arrows in his back, so when his body is found there is no question on how he died and no association will be made with Roger. They watch as the current slowly starts taking the body away. Koawa notices White Horse looking at him. He finally speaks.

"Why didn't you tell me?" he says.

"Tell you what?" Koawa asks. White Horse just smiles.

"My brother, have you forgotten? My feet were swept away from a beautiful White Woman as well."

Koawa ignores him and finishes watching Rupert's body float away.

"Have you kissed her?" White Horse asks.

"Will you stop," Koawa says annoyed. White Horse is not fooled. He knows his brother well.

"Why haven't you? It is obvious you want to."

Koawa huffs. He loves his brother to death, but sometimes he can be so annoying. "Because she is different," he answers.

"Hmm," White Horse says. "I think you are afraid of losing her if you move too fast. I understand, that is the same concern I had when I fell for my Prairie Dawn."

"How long did you wait?" Koawa asks.

"I don't remember exactly, but I had a thirst to taste her lips of honey the first time I saw her." Koawa nods his head yes as he feels the same way.

"She is very beautiful," White Horse says. Koawa nods his head in agreement.

"Have you given her a name?"

"Sunflower," he answers.

"That is a good name for her," he smiled.

"After Running Water died, I never thought I would love again." Koawa looks over at his brother. "Oh, brother I want her bad and I do not care who knows."

White Horse nods his head, as he can remember how he felt the same way with his Prairie Dawn.

"Invite her to the camp." White Horse teases." I want to talk to the woman who has swept my brother off his feet."

"I can't do that," he answers.

"Why not?"

Koawa knew if he was to take his Sunflower back to his camp, that there would be nothing to stop him from taking her to his pelt. He knows if he keeps her here, then he will be able to control his desires.

"Because she is not safe," he lies.

White Horse is not fooled that is the real reason as to why he doesn't want to take her back to camp, because he too delayed in taking Prairie Dawn back with him for the same reason. He plays along and humors his brother.

"She is safer there than you are here," White Horse says.

"If I take her back brother, there is too much danger for me."

"You can take her back to camp and not take her to your pelt," White Horse says.

Koawa twists his mouth. A habit he has when he is thinking and tempted to do something that he knows he shouldn't.

"No, as much as I want to. I can't right now. Roger has offered his cavern. I will see her there. That way we are both safe."

"Don't take too long brother," White Horse warns, "that kind of beauty will not stay single for long."

Their conversation is stopped when they see Roger approaching.

"She is going to be fine," he says. Going to leave a little mark, but she will be fine."

"Good," White Horse says. Roger looks over at Koawa.

"She is asking for you."

Koawa looks over at White Horse.

"If that was my woman, I wouldn't be standing here." he says.

Koawa grins at his brother. How he admires this man and looks up to him. He is right. He thinks to himself. He will go to her.

"White Horse, I think I have a problem." Roger says.

"What sort of problem?"

"That Doctor had a lot of information on me. Things from the past when you were staying with me when you fell from the falls. He told me that after I left Clarence's bones were found in the flower patch. White Horse, if they track that back they got me."

"Relax brother," White Horse says.

"If Rupert is found, they will put two and two together."

"No, Koawa put arrows in his back and the gash in the back of his head from the tomahawk will just make them believe it was another attack from us. You will have no connection to it all."

Koawa knocks on the door to the bedroom before opening it up and coming in. He sees his Sunflower sitting up reading a book.

"Hi," she grins when she sees him walk in. She reaches her hand out for his. He places his hand into hers and gives it a gentle squeeze.

"My warrior princess," he smiles.

'My knight in shining armor," she smiles back.

"Roger said you will be alright."

"Yes. He wants me to stay here for a few hours just to make sure I don't get dizzy again."

"Good."

"May I ask you a question?"

"Of course." Koawa answers.

"When I was on the floor out there you called me Sunflower."

"Yes," he nods.

"Why?"

"It is the Lakota name that I have given you," he answers.

"Why would you give me one?" she wonders.

"In our culture we would give a name to the one who is very special to us."

"Oh, kind of like how we would do a sweetheart tree," she says.

"What is a sweetheart tree?" Koawa asks confused.

"Oh, you have never heard of it."

"No," he answers.

"It is a huge tree that is greater than most. The person who is sweet on you would carve a heart into the bark with the initials of the person they are sweet on. I never did though, I always thought it was more fun to just climb it."

"Hmm," Koawa says. "It seems kind of foolish. Why did you not just tell them?"

He watches her chuckle. Her laugh is so cute he thinks and her smile lightens up the room. He looks over at the door when he hears movement to see White Horse. He knows it is time to leave.

"I have to leave, but I will be back as soon as I am safe."

"You promise?" she asks. Koawa lifts her hand and kisses it.

"I promise."

Chapter Twenty-Two
An Angered Chief

The trees are starting to change on the Great Plains. The cool days of Autumn are fast approaching. Kikimo went on his vision quest. White Horse and a few of his warriors are camped nearby to watch for any potentials threats while he is on his quest. After three days and two nights, Kikimo was successful in and is now known as Stalking Wolf.

Koawa is making his way to the meadow by the entrance to the cavern where he will wait for his Sunflower. So far, he has been able to avoid contact with the Blue Coat's. One time he had a close call when he was with Stalking Wolf, but they were able to avoid detection when they slid into the cavern from the open crevice in the meadow. It was the first time that Stalking Wolf had seen the cavern.

He has been meeting his Sunflower here for the last few weeks. On their last visit, Sunflower told him she was going to bring a picnic. He has been looking forward to this and has a special gift for her as well. He watches her as she rides up through the meadow. He lifts her off her horse and they embrace before making their way into the cavern. Hand and hand, they make the twists and turns through the corridors until they reach their usual spot at the back of the cavern. Koawa takes his Sunflower's hand and they both sit down across from each other. She starts setting up the picnic.

"I have something for you," he says reaching into this waistline.

"Aww how sweet," she says. Koawa pulls out a necklace that he made her last night.

"Oh, Koawa that is beautiful," she says.

He puts it over her head and watches it fall freely onto her chest. She admires the beauty. "Thank you," she smiles. Koawa strokes her cheek. "This is a special necklace with a meaning behind it."

"What is the meaning of it?"

"It means you are my girl," he smiles, as he twills one of her curls that falls freely with his finger.

"Thank you," she says as she gives him a hug. "I will wear it with pride."

"You need to keep it under your blouse and close to your heart. I do not want anyone else to see it."

"Okay," she says. Koawa watches her tuck the necklace under her blouse. How his heart has grown so fond of her.

"I hope you are hungry?" she asks.

"I am."

He watches her remove the food from the basket. How intoxicated he is by her beauty and her kind soul.

"Do you like killing people and being a warrior?" she asks him.

"Being a warrior is not just killing people. A warrior protects what is of value to them like their home, their family, and their food. It is not about killing other people. We protect what is sacred to us."

"So, you would protect me?"

"In a heartbeat," he says.

He gazes into her eyes as she starts plating his food. She stops what she is doing when he feels his touch on her cheek. She turns her attention to him.

Koawa hesitates, as he is not sure this is the time and he does not want to move too fast and scare her off. They have been talking for several weeks and he just gave her a necklace announcing that she is his girl. He takes the risk, as the desire to taste her lips consumes him. He leans across and kisses her. He is pleased when she welcomes it and kisses him back. When their lips part, he strokes her cheek.

"You are very special to me Sunflower," he says. "Very, very special." She leans her head into his hand and he caresses it. "As you are to me," she says. He gazes at her beauty as she plates his food and then hands it to him.

"I need to give you something now. It is not correct that you give me a gift and I do not give you something in return."

"You already did," he grins.

"What did I give you?" she asks confused.

"A kiss," he grins.

"Would you like another one?" she flirts.

"Very much so," he smiles. He hears her chuckle and then leans in and gives her another kiss.

The rest of their visit they enjoyed their picnic and sat in that cavern for hours, until it was time for each to leave.

The body of Rupert was found ten miles downstream by a local farmer and brought back to the Fort. Roger says that they are not suspicious of him, but are blaming the Sioux for his death, which technically is true. White Horse is still worried about Roger and is growing concerned that Roger's past is catching up to him. He can't shake the feeling that his brother-in-law is being watched. Unfortunately, due to the high risk of an attack and not knowing where the Blue Coats are, White Horse needs his warriors close. So, for that reason he cannot allow his scouts to keep a watch on Roger. He knows that Koawa is seeing Sunflower in the cavern several times a week and knows at least when he is there, that Roger is safe.

Prancing Doe is almost four months old. Betsy, the goat, has been able to provide her with enough milk that she is thriving. Blue Thunder has returned and has become a very good father to Matthew, Little Fox. He has been teaching him his way of life and how to hunt. I have been teaching Little Fox the language and he is starting to catch on. It is not an easy language to learn but he is young and fortunate for him, his vocabulary hasn't matured yet which makes it easier to learn.

Today I am out collecting berries with the other woman. Soon we will not be able to do this as the evenings are already bringing a chill. I fear we are in for an early winter. It is necessary that we collect as much food as we can and preserve it for the winter months as food becomes even more scares during that time.

Morning Dove will be ten years old this year. I remember the day like it was yesterday that she was born. I had not been married to White Horse for very long and was still struggling to be accepted by the Lakota's. Running Water, Morning Dove's mother, left very early one day after an argument with Koawa. After a search for her I found her under a willow tree in active labor. There was no time to get her back to camp and I had to deliver Morning Dove. It was that day that had changed everything for me and my acceptance grew within the tribe.

When Running Water had laid dying in my arms after being shot by a Blue Coat in the back, she made me promise that I would raise Morning Dove as my own and that I would always be there for her beloved Koawa. Before her death Running Water and I had become very close. We both exchanged a necklace that we would wear and upon our deaths we would give that necklace to that spouse. We made a vow to each other that we would watch over and care for them and our children. It is a promise that to this day I have kept. Koawa treasures the necklace and has it hanging over Morning Dove's pelt.

I consider Morning Dove a daughter to me. She is with me everywhere I go and I teach her our customs just as her mother taught me when I first came to live with the Lakota's. Her father and I have become very close friends. Koawa is my backbone. He has rescued me, protected me, and loved me like a brother. There is absolutely nothing I would not do for him.

With Blue Thunder riding along with the hunting party, I have Little Fox with me as well as Morning Dove. Our baskets are nearly full. We are all growing tired as we have been picking for hours. I then notice that Little Fox is no longer within my eyesight. I put down my basket to go find him as I know he cannot be too far. My suspicions are correct when I find him just on the other side of the hill picking berries off another bush.

"There you are," I grin. "Did your father caution you on the danger of running off on your own?" I ask him as I come down to his level. He nods his head yes.

"Then why did you leave?" I ask him.

"The berries were all picked," he says. "So, I came to find some more." It was then that I see what berries he has been picking. I am quick at slapping them out of his hand.

"Did you eat any of these berries?" I ask him.

He failed to answer me and looked as if he was scared. I touch his shoulder to let him know I was not angry with him. He then shakes his head no.

"Good," I answer.

"Mama ate them though," he said. I gasped.

"Little Fox, did your mother eat some of these berries?"

"Yes, she gave me some too and I put them in my pocket but there was a hole in my pocket, and I lost them."

"Oh my God," I mumble. It was then that I was certain I knew how Stella died.

"Little Fox, you must promise me that you will never eat or even touch these berries ever again. As they are beautiful and look divine to eat, they are poisonous and can make you very, very sick and you could even die. You promise?" He nods his head in agreement.

"Good." I then come to stand and take his hand. "Let us go back and join the others and please do not ever take off on your own again."

"I won't," he reassures me.

Early evening is on us. I mentioned to Blue Thunder how I thought Stella may have died. He was grateful that his son did not eat any of the poisonous berries and made a point to reinforce to him how important it was that he never eat them again.

Koawa has returned to camp. He has taken Morning Dove into his lodge with him. Lately he seems different to me. Not the typical hard ass Koawa I know and love. When I question White Horse about it, he just smiled and said that his brother couldn't be better.

I have put Prancing Doe down for the night, so I decide to join White Horse outside our lodge where he is making himself some fresh arrows.

"She finally asleep?" he asks.

"Yes," I answer. "All she wants to do is eat."

"Good," he says. "Let her get extra weight on her for the winter. If I can't find a decent hunt to sustain us, that goat will become dinner."

"Oh, Little Foot would not be happy."

"He is old enough to learn the cycle of life."

White Horse has never been fond of Betsy and only agreed to her because of the milk she produces for his daughter. I know he would not hesitate to put an arrow in her if it came down to feeding his family.

"What would we feed Prancing Doe?" I wonder.

"She would be fine. I would see to it," he answers.

I knew he would. That is one thing that White Horse is and that is a good provider. I may not have the jewels and the coins, but never have I ever felt like I was missing anything. White Horse has always made certain I have never been without.

"White Horse, I miss my brother," I say changing the subject.

"I know darling, but until I know where those Blue Coats are you are not going anywhere." He looks up at me. "I am not going to risk the chance of losing you or him."

"I understand," I sigh.

Our conversation is brought to a stop when we see our eldest son walking up. The expression on his face is radiant. He looks so happy and excited.

"I have something to tell you both," he says. White Horse stops what he is doing and looks up at his son.

"I am a man now," he says.

"We are aware of this," I tell him.

"Well, I am getting married." White Horse and I are both stunned.

"I knew you were sweet on someone," he said, "but it never occurred to me that you were seriously thinking of marriage."

"Oh, I am very serious," he says.

"Who is she son?" I ask.

"Rising Sun," he says. I look down at White Horse and can immediately see his rage. I watch him come to his feet.

"No," he snaps, "I will not allow it."

Stalking Wolf looked at his father in disbelief. He thought for sure that his father would embrace it with open arms.

"Why?" he asks.

"Son," I say. "Perhaps you are going too fast. Give it more time."

"No," he argues.

"You will not marry her," White Horse growls. "You can have anyone else you want but not her."

"You have never liked her!" Stalking Wolf yells. "Because she is Crow."

"That is not why," White Horse says.

"Then why do I not have your blessing?"

"Because you are my son and I am your Chief and I will not allow it in my camp."

"Then maybe we should leave!" he snaps.

I come between the two of them. They are so much alike in so many ways but in the end, I knew the clear winner would be White Horse. I could see how upset he was making our son.

"Son," I say calmly.

"No!" he yells at me.

"You will not talk to her in that tone." White Horse scolds.

"I will marry her and I don't care what you say even if I have to run away. I will do it. You will not stop me father. Never!" He then storms off. I try to run after him.

"Leave him be." White Horse barks.

I look at my husband whose face is stone cold. I knew he was fuming. "You need to tell him the truth," I say.

"No," he barks.

"If you don't tell him, he will marry her."

"I will toss her worthless body back to the Crows before I will allow that to happen."

"You do and your son will go after her. White Horse you have to tell him."

White Horse's eyes were like ice. I have never seen him so angry, especially with me.

"The only reason she is still here is because of you."

"So, this is my fault?" I ask in disbelief. Right now, I am seeing a side of White Horse that I do not like. I turn in disgust to walk away in effort to find my son. White Horse grabs my arm.

"Leave him alone," he growls.

I am usually not afraid of White Horse he has always been very gentle with me and shown nothing but love but right now he was a little intimidating.

"White Horse, you're hurting me," I tell him as I try to free my arm away. His grip becomes stronger.

"You will not go woman," he hisses.

I am a little taken aback by his actions and at this moment I am little frightened. I know if he wanted to, he could really hurt me.

By now all eyes are on us and you could hear a pin drop. Suddenly, I hear Prancing Doe cry. I try to free my arm again.

"White Horse, the baby."

His grip is really starting to hurt and I can feel my arm starting to become numb. I see Medicine Moon rush into our lodge. I am sure it is to calm a crying Prancing Doe. I watch my husband and his stone iced eyes fixed onto mine. I could feel the tears starting to form in my eyes out of pain and fear.

I then see Koawa out of the corner of my eye. I hear him come up behind me and speak his tongue to White Horse telling him to let me go. My eyes are fixed on White Horse who remains with his firm grip on my arm. Koawa places his hand onto White Horse's to get him to release his grip. Koawa, again in a deeper, more threatening tone tells him to let go. He is the only warrior in this band who has ever had the guts to stand up against White Horse. Koawa is completely fearless.

Eventually, White Horse releases his grip on me and Koawa pulls me away. I shake my head at him in disbelief as never has this man ever shown any aggression to me in all the years, I have known him. I rub my tingling arm in total dismay on what has just occurred. Koawa is now next to White Horse, calming him down. I make my quick exit to find my eldest and to get as far away as I can from White Horse.

I find Stalking Wolf by the lake sitting on the hill. I come down to the ground to join him.

"I am sorry I was curt with you," he said.

"It's alright. I understand."

"Why does he hate her so much?" he asks.

"It's a very long story that goes back many years when Red Hawk and your father were boys."

"Ma why did father kill Red Hawk?"

"He had little choice. Trust me son it was not what he wanted to do but what he had to do."

"I don't understand."

"Red Hawk was after me. He tried to kill Koawa when Koawa came to my protection and then he tried to kill your father."

"But why?" I sigh for I believe the truth needs to be known but I am not sure that I am the one who should be saying it.

"Ma why won't anyone tell me? What can be so bad to make father hate Rising Sun? What has she done?"

"Nothing, she is hated because of her mother and Red Hawk. That's the only reason."

"I know father won't tell me, but will you? Please."

"If I tell you we may both be sleeping out here." I smile.

"No, father will always forgive you because to him you are his everything just like Rising Sun is mine."

"Oh," I whine. If he only knew what his father just did, he may rethink that.

"When your grandmother was unable to conceive, she asked your grandfather to go to Running Bears camp and find another wife that could bear his child. He took Yellow Bird. She conceived and that child was Red Hawk. It was shortly after Red Hawk was conceived that your grandmother was blessed with your father."

"So Red Hawk was fathers' brother?"

"Half-brother," I comment. "Your grandfather wanted nothing to do with Red Hawk and that is how he became to live with Running Bear."

"But what does this have to do with Rising Sun?"

"Son, I think that is something that needs to come from your father."

"No!" He will only bully his way to get what he wants and I am not going to allow it. I love Rising Sun and I will make her my wife even if I have to leave camp forever to do it."

"You can't son. Please just take my word for it."

"Father has you against me to." he jeers.

"No one is against you son. We are protecting you."

"Protecting me from what?"

"From making the worse mistake in your life."

Stalking Wolf jumps to his feet. "You don't understand. I will marry her!" He yells.

"Stop!" I yell. "You can't marry her."

"Give me one good reason why."

"She is your half-sister."

Stalking Wolf stopped in his tracks. He shook his head in disbelief. "No," he says, "You're lying."

"I wish I was. It's true. Rising Sun is your half-sister that is why you cannot marry her."

"No!" he yells. "No!" he then and runs off.

"Kikimo!" I yell as I watch him run out of sight.

Chapter Twenty-Three
The Runaway's

Darkness is heavy across the land. Little Foot is staying the night with Blue Thunder and Little Fox leaving me alone in my thoughts. I am in our lodge putting a restless Prancing Doe back to sleep. I had just accomplished this task when the flap to my lodge opens and White Horse steps in. I apprehensively watch him, as he stops a moment and looks at me. I wasn't sure if I should be afraid of him or pity him. He comes closer to me and takes my hand. He lifts it to his lips and kisses it.

I do not know what to say," he says. "What I did to you is shameful. I hurt the one person who I vowed that I would never hurt."

My heart was aching. I wipe a tear that is starting to fall. White Horse catches it with his thumb.

"My love, I plead that you will forgive me."

"Why?" I wonder. "What made you snap?"

"I was afraid you were going to tell our son the truth. I couldn't let you do it."

"You were right," I say. "He knows that Rising Sun is his sister."

"Carrie," he huffs. "I wish you hadn't"

"He needed to know White Horse, why we were so against it."

"How did he take it?" he sighs.

"Not well. I did not tell him how it all came about just that she was his sister. I am sure his mind is racing on how."

For a few moments White Horse is speechless. I watch him sit down on his pelt. He pushes his hair back over his forehead, something I have noticed he does when he is frustrated with his lack of words. Finally, he speaks.

"Well, he will hate for me awhile, but in time he will understand at least now he won't marry her."

"You sure about that White Horse?" I question.

"Yes, he is a smart boy. He will break it off."

I was not as confident as White Horse was. He reaches up his hand for me to take it. I love this man with all my heart. I do not like what he did to me and it better never happen again, because as much as I love him, I will not tolerate any aggressiveness. I take his hand and come down to the pelt beside him. He looks at the massive bruise that has already formed on my arm. He lowers his head in shame. I heard a sniff from him. He was truly upset about what he had done. I honestly believe he is remorseful. He places his hand on my shoulder.

"My Prairie Dawn will you ever forgive me?"

I am still baffled at how quickly he turned on me and how aggressive he became. I am not sure what would have happened if Koawa had not intervened. It is clear to me that White Horse still has so much anger inside him from his past that he somehow needs to find peace with. I can only pray that this is an isolated incident, as we have been married for nearly ten years and he has never once showed anything but love to me. I squeeze his hand.

"My Chief, oh how I love you. Being angry with you is such a waste," I smile.

I can tell by his grin that he is relieved. He gently pulls me down onto the pelt and comes on top of me where he would shower me with kisses. He promised me that he would never touch me in that way again and all his love for me would be gentle. As the night progresses, White Horse makes up on every wrong he did by pleasing me with his tongue and then riding me until we were too exhausted to continue.

Another afternoon crosses the land. Roger is in the cavern. He heard Koawa and Corrine come in earlier and make their way to the back of the cavern into a back corridor. He has been studying the map for some time. He looks at the funny circles that go through this squiggly line. He is pretty sure that the squiggly line must be the stream. He follows the stream through the cavern looking at the water for anything that may resemble the circles on the map. He spots three rocks that are oddly shaped clustered next to each other. He examines the map.

"That has to be a clue to something," he says to himself.

He steps out into the shallow stream and picks up one of the rocks. He quickly sees that it is not your normal rock but is a gold nugget.

"Earl had to have put them here," he thinks to himself. He looks at the map again and then at the rocks. He concludes that they are a land marker of some sort. Roger is convinced Earl has something hidden of value in this cavern, but of what he is clueless.

The cavern is huge and has many twists and turns. It is damp, dark, and eerie in many of the corridors. Some that lead to nowhere and others that lead to other corridors. If Earl had hidden something here it could be lost forever. Roger studies the map in detail and is in hard concentration. He is unaware of movement coming up behind him. He jumps when a hand rests on his shoulder. Roger is quick at turning around to see the face of his nephew Stalking Wolf.

"Oh, you gave me a start," he says.

"Sorry Leksi, I didn't mean to scare you."

"What are you doing here?" Roger asks.

"I want you to meet someone," he says.

He motions for Rising Sun to come out. Roger sees her coming out carrying a child on her hip.

"Leksi, this is Rising Sun, my wife."

Roger was still a moment from the shock, before reaching out his hand to welcome her. She failed to take it back.

"She doesn't trust a lot of people."

"I see, well I guess congratulations are in order."

"Thank you," Stalking Wolf smiles.

"But I must admit I am a little hurt I was not invited to the ceremony."

"We did not have a ceremony. Father was against us getting married, so we left. In Lakota custom a couple is considered married if they leave together for a certain number of days. In a few more days we will be married by our law and there is nothing that Father can do about it."

"I see," Roger says. "Kikimo..." Stalking Wolf holds out his hand to correct his uncle.

"My apologies," Roger says, "Stalking Wolf," he corrects. "Why are you here?"

"Because Father will see that we are gone and will start looking for us, so we came here. I know Little Fox is at the camp with Little Foot. Sleeping Bear needs a nap and I was hoping Rising Sun could put him to sleep on his bed. It will only be for one night, Uncle, I promise. Tomorrow we are moving on.

"Of course, you can. You are welcomed here as long as you wish, but you will need to put your horse in the barn."

"Thank you Leski," Stalking Wolf says giving him a hug. "I knew I could count on you."

"Well why don't you put your horse in the barn and I will take Rising Sun with me and we will get Sleeping Bear some milk."

"Okay," Stalking Wolf translates to Rising Sun the plan and helps her up the ladder to the crawl space over the fireplace that leads into the house.

"Oh," Roger says snapping his fingers." I almost forgot something. I will be right back. You go ahead and I will be right there."

Roger waits until the ladder is clear before making his way to the back of the cavern. He will make several turns until he finds Koawa in a small corridor. He finds him and Sunflower sitting across from each other holding hands and talking. Koawa looks at him when he enters.

"I am sorry to disturb you," he says.

"What is it?"

"Kikimo is here. Apparently, him and White Horse had an argument and he has run away."

Koawa rolls his eyes, as he deeply sighs. He leans in and kisses Sunflower.

"I will be right back." He tells her and comes to his feet.

White Horse is fuming over his son running away. He knows his son will not chance going far, because of the Blue Coats, especially when he has a child with them. He is pretty sure he knows where he is. He is heading that way with Blue Thunder and Grey Wolf beside him.

Koawa finds his nephew and has him by his tunic and pushing him through the corridors. He plops him down on the ground in front of Sunflower. He then takes his place beside her against the wall of the cavern and entwines his fingers through hers. She in return rested her head down on his shoulder.

"Sunflower, this is my nephew Kikimo."

"Stalking Wolf!" he corrects.

"Stalking Wolf." Koawa snaps. "I do not think you saw your vision clear. Stalking Wolf is a man's name. You are just a child."

"I am so a man!" he yells.

"A real man doesn't run away from his problems. He faces them like a true warrior." Stalking Wolf lowers his eyes.

"Now why did you run away?" Koawa asks.

"Father prohibits me to marry Rising Sun."

Koawa just looks at his nephew shaking his head at the stupidity of the boy. How he reminds him of his Father at that age, arrogant and pig headed. "You are just like your Father," he says.

"I am nothing like my Father." Stalking Wolf barks.

"Yes, you are," he chuckles. "You are both arrogant and foolish."

"You better not let Father hear you call him foolish," Stalking Wolf warns.

"Go home." Koawa says.

"No," he argues.

Koawa has had enough of his unruly nephew. His little fit is interfering with the time he desires to spend with his Sunflower. Koawa leans his head into hers. How he loves the way she smells. The way it makes his insides melt. For a few moments he just stares at his nephew.

"Do you know why your Father never told you the truth?" Koawa finally says.

"No."

"He was protecting you."

"From what?"

"The Crows."

"The Crows?" Stalking Wolf questions.

"Yes."

"What do the Crows have to do with it?"

"They are our enemies and back when this happened, they were very dominant and feared, even by us. Your Father had to keep his secret so you would live. Kikimo if you were to marry her, it could get very ugly for him. I do not think you want to put that kind of pain on your mother."

"Mother said she is my half-sister."

"Yes, this is true," Koawa says.

"But I don't understand why Red Hawk raised her if she is Crow?"

"Because there is Lakota in her blood and he wanted to smear her in your Father's face. Red Hawk was a very dangerous man."

Koawa lifts up his tunic to show his nephew the deep scar he has from when he was stabbed by Red Hawk and nearly died. Corrine gasped. Koawa squeezes her hand.

"Almost, he said, he almost got me. He would have kidnapped your mother and that is why we fought. It was Red Hawk who pushed your Father off the falls that day. He was a very bitter man and very dangerous."

Stalking Wolf is in disbelief. "But what does this have to do with Rising Sun?"

"Kikimo, all you need to know is your Father did what he had to do to protect you. I know you love her, but you cannot marry her." Koawa watches as his nephew's eyes weld up.

He can tell that his nephew really does love her. He also knows that he is his brother's son and he knows his brother would not hold back his urge when it came to a beautiful woman.

"Have you laid with her?" he asks.

"Yes," he sheepishly says.

Koawa is not pleased with what he heard. A faint curse word is spoken in his tongue. He tries to compose himself by repositioning his body and gently squeezing Sunflower's hand. For a few seconds he speaks not a word, as he stares his nephew down.

"Part of being a warrior is learning to control your urges," he starts, "when you love a woman, you treat her with respect. You can show a woman how much you love her, that does not require you to take her to your pelt. Making love to a woman son, is a very magical connection and one you do not take lightly and never should it be done out of wedlock, because that is very disrespectful to her."

Stalking Wolf looks over at Sunflower. She is such a beautiful woman, almost as beautiful as his mother. He can see why his uncle has fallen for her. He can see the love that his uncle has for her, it is a pure and deep love. He knew he was wrong. He never should have done what he did and he never should have left home.

"What do I tell my Father?" he asks.

"The truth. Your Father is not an unreasonable man. You must respect his wishes, as you know deep down he is correct. I just hope it is not too late and the seed isn't already planted."

"How do I let her go?"

"It is hard to let go of something that you love, but it has to be done."

"I want to go home," Stalking Wolf whines.

Koawa smiles. Finally, he thinks his nephew is making some sense.

"Where will Rising Sun go?" Stalking Wolf asks.

"That is up to your father." Koawa answers as he takes Sunflower's hand and comes to a stand. "I will take you as far as the scouts. Go get what you need and let your uncle know you are leaving."

"Okay."

Koawa watches his nephew leave. He then turns to Sunflower. "That was about the sweetest thing I have ever heard," she says. Koawa smiles down into her beautiful eyes.

"I am sorry I have cut our visit short," he tells her.

"I understand. I need to get back as well. My brother is starting to get suspicious as to where I keep going. Just let me tell Roger goodbye."

Hand in hand they walk through the cavern. Koawa waits at the bottom of the ladder to make sure his love gets safely up. When she is all clear, he then makes his way to the crevice where he will slip out into the meadow and go meet up with the scouts.

Chapter Twenty-Four
The Arrest

Corrine has made her way through the crawl space and is stepping out into the loft. Stalking Wolf grabs her hand to help her to her feet.

"Thank you," she says. She sees a baby asleep on the bed and a young Indian girl sitting beside it.

"This is Rising Sun," Stalking Wolf greets.

"What a beautiful name," she smiles.

Corrine makes her way to the stairs.

"He is a good man," Stalking Wolf says.

"Who is?" she asks.

"My uncle. He will treat you well."

She smiles over at him slightly blushing, before making her way down the stairs. She sees Roger at his desk studying the map.

"You have been glued to that thing all day," she says.

"I am determined to figure this out. I would like to know exactly how wealthy I am," he jokes.

"Do you mind if I grab some water before I leave?"

"Of course not. I just filled the pitcher. Help yourself."

Koawa has made his way through the small crevice that leads to the meadow where he left his horse to graze. He picks up its lead and is about ready to jump on its back, when a small breeze crosses his face. He takes a whiff of the fresh air and then panic consumes him. "Sunflower," he says. He then runs.

"Did Koawa talk to his nephew?" Roger wonders.

"Yes, he did. The boy is going home."

"Good. I put Max in the barn so he wouldn't follow you."

"Thank you."

Suddenly Corrine and Roger both jump when the door comes flying open. General Phillips is the first through the door, followed by his soldiers in command. Roger is quickly apprehended by two soldiers who are restraining him by his arms. Roger knew what was coming.

"Get out of here!" Roger yells at Corrine. Corrine runs to the stairs, but is quickly captured.

The General glares over at Roger. He tosses Roger's journal down on the table.

"Does this look familiar?" he growls.

In the haste to leave White Horses camp to slow down Custer, Roger not only forgot his medical bag, but he forgot to pick up his journal as well. He takes a deep sigh, as he knows the charade is up. He is then hit in the stomach with the butt of a rifle. He bellows in pain.

"Doctor Briggs," General Phillips says. "I hereby place you under arrest for treason to the United States Army on aiding the escape of the enemy."

"That is no proof!" Roger yells.

"I have the witness testimony from the sister and my adopted son of seeing you with the Chief at the orphanage. I have a written statement from the sheriff at your last employment of human remains found in the flower bed at your old homestead, that I am certain belongs to a shopkeeper that went missing. I have numerous eyewitness encounters from Willow Creek of your sister leaving with a Lakota Chief after their town went under siege from renegade Indians. The same Chief that you have written about in your journal. This is all the proof needed to see you dangling from a noose." Roger grew still as he knows he cannot talk his way out of this.

"You have been helping them escape for years." The General growls. "I am personally going to enjoy seeing you hang."

The General looks over at the soldier who has Roger by his arm. "Get him out of here."

A soldier who has Corrine by the arm asks, "And what about the lady sir?"

"You leave her alone," Roger yells, "she has nothing done wrong."

"Aiding and abetting is a crime," the General states.

Corrine lets out a scream. "No! let me go."

She is no match for the soldier and is quickly subdued. Eyes then turn to Roger who is hit with another blow to the stomach.

Stalking Wolf has heard everything from on top of the stairs. He whips out his knife and lunges down the steps on top of a soldier's back that is holding Corrine. He begins to stab him. The soldier bellows in pain. A shot is heard hitting Stalking Wolf in the back. He falls forward to the ground dead.

A beaten Roger is in horror as he sees his nephew lying dead in a pool of blood. He then is pistol whipped on the back of his head and is knocked out cold.

Koawa has made his way up the ladder and starting to crawl through the turn around the fireplace. He looks through the cracks and sees his nephew lying in a pool of blood. "Sunflower," he says and he hastily finishes his crawl to the loft and down the stairs. He comes over to his nephew. His heart saddens. He hears Rising Sun crying, as she cowards in the corner. Just then White Horse, Grey Wolf, and Blue Thunder come running through the opened front door. White Horse stops dead in his tracks upon seeing his son in a pool of blood.

"No!" he cries out.

Koawa is frantic as he is not seeing his Sunflower anywhere. He runs to the door and looks out. He sees that her horse is still here. He rushes over to Rising Sun.

"Where is she?" he says. Rising Sun continues to cry. Koawa shakes her. "Answer me!" he yells.

"The soldiers came and they took her and Great Healer. Stalking Wolf tried to stop them and they shot him."

White Horse glares over at her. His eyes are of ice. The veins in his neck are pulsating. He grabs her and violently shakes her. "You killed him," he roars.

"No," she cries. "The soldiers did."

"He would not have been here if it wasn't for you. Go!" he roars, pointing to the door. Rising Sun is shaking in fear, as tears are rolling down her eyes.

"Go!" White Horse roars, "and if I ever see you again, I will destroy you!"

Rising Sun looks at a stone faced Chief. She is filled with fear, as she knows how violent this man can be. She reaches to pick up Sleeping Bear, who is sitting in the corner near her. White Horse comes between her and the child.

"Get out!" he roars.

When she attempts to go to Sleeping Bear again, White Horse lunges forward in a threatening manner making her jump. She knows she is no match to the angered Chief. With tears streaming down her cheeks, she leaves. Blue Thunder follows her out to make sure she does not return.

White Horse is full of rage and is trying to calm himself down. He sees Koawa grab Roger's rifle over the fireplace and head to the door.

"No!" White Horse barks, chasing after him. He looks at a very irate Koawa.

"They have my Sunflower. I am getting her. You want to join me that's fine, but do not get in my way," Koawa snaps.

"Brother I am full of rage too, but if you go in there and start blowing things up and shooting, both Roger and Sunflower are dead."

"I will not sit back and do nothing when they have my Sunflower," he snarls.

White Horse points over at the lifeless body of his oldest son.

"Look at what they did. Do you honestly think I am going to sit back and do nothing?" He comes straight into Koawa's face.

"You want to see your Sunflower again then calm down and let me think," he barks grabbing the rifle out of Koawa's hand and tossing it on the ground.

He walks back over to his son. Why? He asks himself, why couldn't he just be still? Why was he always in such a hurry to grow up and be the best? He thinks of his Prairie Dawn, who will be shattered by the loss and who will most likely blame him for their son running way in the first place. White Horse tries to keep himself together, even though he is hurting deeply with such a great loss.

"We are taking my son home to his mother," he says. "Then we will return to the meadow and think how to get them out of there, unharmed. Are you with me?" White Horse looks over at Koawa. "Because brother I need my best friend and partner beside me."

"One day," Koawa says. "You have one day to get her out of there and if she is harmed in any way I will start my own war without you."

The people in the Fort are in disbelief when they see their Doctor and Corrine being brought in by General Phillips and his brigade. Gasps are heard when they witness firsthand the shape their doctor is in, as he is being dragged in by two soldiers, because he is too weak from his beatings to walk.

Corrine is escorted to a jail cell and watches in horror, as Roger is tossed on the jail cot like a sack of potatoes. Corrine rushes to help Roger, when she is grabbed by the arm by a soldier.

"Get your hands off me!" she huffs.

"Soldier," the General says, "leave her alone." The soldier backs off.

"Now I want some answers from you pretty lady." The General starts. "I will ask the courts to go easy on you if you cooperate."

"I have nothing to say," she snaps.

"Treason is a hefty sentence even for a woman."

"I don't know what you are talking about."

Just then the General notices Koawa's necklace buried under her collar around her neck. He lifts it out and she grabs it.

He glares over at her with hollow eyes and then smacks her across the face. The force of it pushes her off her feet.

"Get that Indian whore out of here," he says.

Corrine is then brought to her feet and pushed into the jail cell. It is then locked behind her. The General glares through the bars.

"You are a disgrace." He then walks away.

Two armed guards are stationed outside the jail and one inside. Corrine rushes over to Roger, who is badly beaten. She buries her head down on his chest and cries.

White Horse enters the Lakota camp along with his brother-in-law's dog Max, running alongside of him. The body of his son is draped over Spirit Dog's back. He has had the entire ride home to allow his son's senseless death to soak in. He thinks of Koawa, who is out for blood and worries he is not thinking clearly, because of his fear from the woman that he loves. His mind then goes to his Prairie Dawn who he is certain will be devastated and furious with him for the loss of their son. His lodge is in view in the center of the camp. He sees his Prairie Dawn washing clothes at the creek. She watches him as he enters the camp. It did not take her long to see that something was wrong.

I watch my husband as he makes his slow walk through the camp. My heart races with joy, as I know my oldest must be with him. It wasn't until he was closer that my heart flips. I see being led behind him a warrior draped over Spirit Dog's back. I gasp as we have lost one of our warriors. I then notice that Grey Wolf is holding Sleeping Bear, as he rides alongside of his Chief. I find this odd and am curious as to where Rising Sun is. I watch as White Horse gets off a few feet from me. I notice he has a very drawn face.

"White Horse," I say, as he stops in front of me holding the lead to his own pony. I look over at the fallen warrior and immediately my eyes tear up.

"No!" I scream. White Horse attempts to console me.

"No!" I yell.

The realization of who has died has filled the camp and many tears are heard throughout. Minoke rushes to Stalking Wolf. She lifts his head and a loud cry is heard. She follows behind Koawa, who has lifted his nephew off the horse and carries him away.

"Carrie," White Horse says, "the Army has your brother. I must leave to find him and bring him back."

My tears are heavy with the great loss that has been brought upon me. My heart aches and my anger intensify. I blame all this on White Horse.

"You and your damn bruised ego!" I scream.

"What do you mean?" he barks.

"You could not stand the idea of your reputation being tattered or torn. You had to remain on your pedestal."

White Horse understands that his Prairie Dawn is upset and emotions are high, but he refuses to take the blame for his son's death.

"My ego?" he spats, "you are blaming me for my son's death?"

"He never would have run away if you had been honest with him years ago. But Lord forbid, if your damn ego gets bruised."

"Our son was shot in the back by a soldier. The same soldiers that have arrested your brother. Our son died trying to protect his uncle. You want to blame someone then you blame them."

"I knew one day that Roger helping you would get him in trouble. I begged you not to do it. Your arrogance and ego have killed my son and if it kills my brother, I will never forgive you."

White Horse watches as his Prairie Dawn rushes off, wiping her tears as she goes. He has never seen his Prairie Dawn so angry with him and never has she talked to him that way. He knows that she is grieving with the sudden loss of Stalking Wolf. He would normally go after her and give her what comfort he could, but he is certain that right now he is the last person she would want comfort from. He too is grieving his son's loss, but if he doesn't act fast, she could also lose her brother. He gathers his best warriors and together they leave to go get Roger.

Jackson stops in front of the jail and demands to see his sister. The General allows the short visit. He enters the jail and finds his sister curled up on the jail floor. She rushes to him, reaching her arms through the bars and holding his hand. He notices the red marks on her cheek from being slapped.

"I don't have much time. The General told me that you are being charged with treason. What the hell Corrine?"

"Jackson, listen to me," she whispers. She glances over at the soldiers standing at the entrance of the jail. "I need you to go get Koawa for me."

"What the hell Corrine," he yells.

"Jackson hush. I will explain everything later. I promise. I need you to get us out of here."

"How am I going to do that?" Corrine removes Koawa's necklace and hands it to him. "Put this in your pocket, Hurry." Jackson does as he is instructed.

"Go to Roger's home. Follow the creek to the meadow. There you will find Koawa. Show him this. He will know that it came from me. Tell him that tomorrow Roger and I will be on a stagecoach to Fort Lamarie. Roger will be hung." Jackson's eyes grew huge.

"Corrine what have you gotten yourself involved in?"

"We don't have time for that now. Trust me Jackson. Go to him. He will know what to do?" She squeezes his hands.

"Corrine, are you sure he can be trusted to get you out?"

"Jackson, he has saved my life twice. I completely trust him."

Jackson cannot believe what he is hearing.

"Okay you," they hear a soldier say, "times up."

Corrine looks over at her brother. He sees him nod his head in agreement. She faintly smiles. Jackson exits the jail and makes his way to the meadow.

Chapter Twenty-Five
The Escape

Jackson is riding hard across the plains. His mind is doing circles trying to understand how his sister got into this mess. She has always been free spirited and spunky since they were children and she has always played by her own rules, but Treason is something he cannot imagine she would ever do. They have always been extremely close and he trusts his sister with his life. That is why he has agreed to meet up with this Koawa.

He is baffled as to why his sister never mentioned to him about these Indians. When and how did she meet them and how does she know this one she called Koawa? He turns his horse to the road that leads to Roger's and finds the small cabin tucked into the bluff. He follows the creek, as he was instructed to do until he comes to a huge meadow. He abruptly comes to a stop when he sees on top of a hill that he is being watched.

Jackson is pulled off his horse by Grey Wolf and tossed to the ground. Cowering in the tall grass, he sheepishly holds up the necklace. He feels the warrior yank it out of his hand. He lifts his eyes up at Grey Wolf, fearing that at any moment he will be killed. Grey Wolf grabs him by the collar and forces him to his feet. He is then dragged to the edge of the meadow to the cavern wall. He is then tossed down like a rag doll. Grey Wolf shows the necklace to Koawa.

"We found him entering the meadow by the way of Great Healer's place. He showed me this," he said.

Koawa is quick at grabbing it out of his hand. He immediately recognized it. He hands it to White Horse, who also knew whose it was.

"Who are you?" Koawa growls.

"My name is Jackson. My sister Corrine sent me."

Koawa's ears perked up.

"Where is she?" he demands.

"She is at the Fort jail with the Doctor. She told me to come to the one named Koawa, that he could help her."

"That's me," Koawa says.

Koawa looks down at the one who claims to be the brother to his Sunflower. He sees little family resemblance and wonders if this is a trap.

"Corrine and I have spent many hours together and I know her very well. Tell me something about her."

"She likes to fish. Her mother died when she was twelve from fever. She would climb the sweetheart tree after school." Koawa knew he was telling the truth. He helps Jackson to his feet.

"How are you involved with my sister?" Jackson asks.

"Her and I are very close." Koawa says.

"How close?"

Koawa wasn't sure where this was going and does not feel this is the correct time to tell Jackson that he is in love with his sister.

"Close enough that she asked you to come to me for help," he answers.

"Are you the reason she is in there?" Jackson asks.

"No, but I am the one who will get her out."

White Horse comes over to Jackson.

"I am Chief White Horse from a Lakota band that is camped just south of here. That Doctor is my wife's brother and our Great Healer. I want to know what the General has planned for them."

"They are both scheduled to leave on a stagecoach in the morning to Fort Lamarie where the Doctor will be hung and I don't know what will happen to my sister."

"Has she been hurt?" Koawa asks.

"She was slapped pretty hard, but she seems alright."

Instant rage consumes Koawa. White Horse pats him on the back to calm him down. Jackson looks over at the Chief.

"The Doctor was beaten very bad."

White Horse thinks a moment. "How many are guarding the jail?"

"Three, Two outside and one inside."

"I am going!" Koawa growls.

"Wait!" White Horse says.

"I wait no more. I am going to get her out of there," he snaps.

"You go in there attacking, you will get them both killed. We have to be smart with this. We will go in tonight when the Fort is dark."

Koawa is not happy and does not like the idea of his Sunflower being in there for another minute, but he knows his brother is right.

"How far is the jail from the gate?" White Horse asks.

"Not too far. It is right across the street from the General Store." White Horse speak his tongue to Koawa.

"Think we can trust him?" he asks Koawa.

Koawa nods his head yes. White Horse knows Koawa does not trust anyone, so for him to say he can be trusted brings him some comfort.

"If you truly want to get my sister out of there, then I can get you in," Jackson says. "I own the General Store."

"It is not the getting in that is the problem." White Horse says. "It is the getting out."

"Chief, if I may make a suggestion," Jackson says. White Horse is all ears.

"There is a shift change around mid-night. There is only one guard stationed on the wall and only one at the jail. I can meet you on the inside with my wagon. You and the doctor can take cover in the back of the wagon and I can ride you right out."

"Why would you risk your neck for us?" White Horse asks.

"I am doing it for my sister," he answers."

"And you think we will be able to ride right out?"

"I know the soldier at the gate. We are very good friends. I will just tell him I have to get an early start to make a delivery at Hedge Brooke. He will not question it because I do it frequently."

"That could work," White Horse mumbles.

"As for getting Corrine out, I know of a place where there is a break in the wall. You will have to climb on the platform, but after that it is a jump down. Corrine has climbed it before, she will know how to do it. Koawa will just have to lift her up on the platform." Koawa was eager to agree.

"Good," White Horse smiles. He puts his hand on Jackson's shoulder. "You did good my friend."

"For some reason my sister trusts you. She is a very smart woman and very brave." Koawa agrees. Jackson looks over at Koawa. "She is especially fond of you." Koawa grins. "But I don't care how strong she may think she is. She had fear in her eyes and that scares me."

"Corrine speaks very highly of you," Koawa says. "I will get her out of there. This I promise you."

"I don't know how you know my sister, but when I went to see her, she was adamant that I would go to you. I only agreed to come, because I fear for her life."

"So do I." Koawa says.

"Corrine will never be able to return to this life. The General is a brutal man and he does not care that she is a woman. He will see her dead and if the General suspects me, I may be as well. I need to know that she is safe."

"Meet me back here at this time in three days. I will bring her and you can see for yourself."

Darkness has crossed the land. White Horse and Koawa are making their way to the Fort. The plan is as follows. Koawa and White Horse will sneak into the Fort by climbing over the wall. They will kill and steal the jailers key and unlock the jail cell. White Horse will meet up with Jackson and hide in the back of his wagon with Roger and ride out of the Fort. Koawa will take Corrine and they will sneak out the same way that Koawa came in. They all will then meet further out the gate and make a run home. White Horse's scouts will be hiding on the outside of the gate to fight off any soldiers, in the event that things don't go as planned.

With the plan in motion, White Horse and Koawa begin making their way through the crack in the wall and wait under the wooden platform for the guard to pass. Once clear, it was only a few more feet and they were in the Fort. They slither their way through the street until they get to the back of the jail. White Horse looks across the street and sees Jackson and his covered wagon.

The warriors sneak around to the front of the jail and see the guard sitting outside the door asleep. Koawa does the honors on slitting his throat and stealing the keys. The door to the jail is then opened and with no guard inside it was easy access to the cell. Koawa fiddles with the keys, before finding the correct one to unlock it. White Horse wastes no time and lifts Roger onto his shoulders. Koawa squats down to a sleeping Sunflower and nudges her awake. Upon seeing him, she rushes into his arms.

"Shh," he whispers, "let's get you out of here."

Jackson motions to White Horse that it safe to cross the street. White Horse then bolts across jumping into the back of the wagon. Jackson places a blanket over both Roger and White Horse and then positions some empty crates in front of them to make it appear that the wagon is full. He then gets on the front and makes his way to the entrance.

Koawa is holding Sunflower's hand and guiding her along keeping very low and quiet. He gets to the wall and lifts her up onto the platform. She quickly looks around to make sure the coast is clear. Then Koawa pulls himself up and they make their way to the last short jump off the wall, into the prairie grass below.

Jackson is at the gate and talking to the guard. White Horse lays motionless next to Roger. Roger begins to moan. White Horse rolls his body on top of Roger to keep him quiet, as he listens to the conversation outside. He then feels the wagon start to move. They made it he thinks and they are almost clear. He then hears a gunshot and the team of horses begin to gallop out the gate.

Koawa and Sunflower jump off the platform and as soon as they do, Sunflower is spotted. A soldier takes aim and Sunflower is hit in the leg. She screams in pain as she falls to the ground. Koawa shields her, as he tosses his tomahawk at the soldier and it lands in his chest. The Fort is now coming alive with soldiers and they are all racing in the direction of Koawa. Koawa has Sunflower shielded in a hollow in the high prairie grass. He whips out his knife and tosses it at an approaching soldier, landing it in his heart. The Lakota warriors are then seen coming into view.

Koawa picks Sunflower up in his arms and makes a run for it.

White Horse has made it to his horse and has Roger draped over it. He is waiting for Koawa to arrive. White Horse grows concerned when he hears the gun shots and Koawa has not appeared. He hears his warriors storming the Fort. Suddenly, he sees Koawa come into his view.

"They hit her?" he asks.

"In the leg," he answers, while lifting her up and putting her on his horse.

"I don't know where Jackson went," White Horse says.

"He can take care of himself," Sunflower says.

The Lakota warriors are heard leaving. That is a sign to White Horse that the soldiers are following them. He knows his men will only temporarily be able to keep them away and he has no time to waste before the General realizes that Roger is not with them. White Horse looks up at the sky. "I hope this storm holds off until we get home."

Koawa, who is on his horse, looks at White Horse.

"If we don't leave now, we will have a bigger storm to worry about."

Chapter Twenty-Six

The Fugitives

Thunder is rolling and the wind is picking up as White Horse and Koawa guide their horses through the trees on a moonless night. They are being extremely quiet, as they are certain that the soldiers have realized that both Roger and Corrine are missing and not with the war party that they are chasing. It is just a matter of time before they regroup and expand their search for the fugitives. Roger is starting to wake up, forcing White Horse to stop. Koawa slides off the back of his horse. He gently squeezes Sunflower's hand. "I will be right back. I need to help White Horse with Roger," he tells her.

Koawa approaches White Horse, as he is lifting Roger off his horse.

"I do not think the storm or him will last until we get home," he says.

"We can go back to the cavern," Koawa says.

"No," White Horse says. "That will be the first place they will look and the meadow is too close. I will not chance it."

"Brother, I don't know of any caves near here."

"I don't either," he says. "How is Sunflower doing?"

221

"She is doing alright. I just don't like the way her leg looks."

"Help me lift Roger up in front of me," he says. "We will stay in the trees and head up into the hills and if any luck the storm will wash away our tracks."

Koawa lifts Roger up and helps sit him in front of White Horse. Roger is leaning so White Horse has to put one arm around him, so he doesn't fall off, as he guides in his horse through the trees.

It is then that they hear horses approaching. White Horse is quick at galloping up a hill and disappearing into the darkness of the trees. Koawa has no time to mount, so he grabs his horse's lead and runs into the trees. He reaches up and hastily grabs Sunflower off her horse, smacking its behind and it runs off. He then races her to the tall grass where he will lay on top of her.

Koawa hears the horses approaching. He removes his knife from his sheave and is ready to pounce. He can feel his Sun flower's heart racing through his tunic. He knows she is terrified. Koawa had no time to cover their tracks. He worries if the soldiers have an experienced Indian scout with them, that even though they are covered in nearly complete darkness that they would be able to pick it up.

His stance becomes defensive when he hears the horses stop. He hears his Sunflower's breathing become harder. He looks down into her scared eyes. He kisses her forehead reassuring her that everything will be alright. He then hears the horses leave. He waits for a few seconds before lifting his head out of the tall grass. He sees the back end of the six horses walking away. He comes out of the grass when he sees White Horse approaching, with his pony being led behind him. He goes to his Sunflower, who he can tell is still very frightened. He wraps his arms around her and carries her to his horse.

"I thought we lost your horse," she says in a light humor.

"He is trained," Koawa says when he jumps on behind her. "He will never stray far from me."

"That was too close," White Horse says. "We have to find a place to take shelter for the night for this storm is coming in quick and Great Healer is not going to make it much further."

"The old Hanson place," Sunflower says. "It has been abandoned for years."

"Do you know where it is?" Koawa asks.

"Yes. I don't think it is much further."

"Show me," Koawa says.

The old Hanson place is seen off in the distance. White Horse and Koawa bring their horses to stop just when the skies begin to open.

"Stay here," Koawa tells Sunflower. "I need to check it out."

Corrine watches as Koawa runs into the small house. She thinks how much she loves this man and how loved he makes her feel. She then looks over at the Chief. She remembers the story that Koawa told her on how he became a Chief at such a young age and wonders if it is a blessing or a curse. She notices how exceptionally handsome he is, even in the darkness of the night. She finds Koawa very soothing on the eyes, but this Chief is breathtakingly stunning.

"I am sorry about your son," she says. White Horse turns his eyes to her and faintly nods his head.

"He saved my life," she said. "I just wanted you to know that."

"What did he do?" he wonders.

"A soldier had me on the floor. Your son jumped on his back and started stabbing him. It was enough that I was able to break free. That is when one of the other soldiers shot him."

For a moment White Horse was still. The pain from the death of his son still very raw to him.

"Thank you," he finally says. "It will help his mother find peace knowing he died a hero."

She then sees Koawa running towards them.

"It's clear and I think the soldiers have already been here. I picked up some tracks by the door."

"Good," White Horse says. "Hopefully they won't be back." Koawa walks over to his horse, removing the blanket.

"I will be right back for you," he says. "I need to help White Horse get Roger inside."

"I can get myself in," she says.

"No honey, I don't want you standing on that leg," he argues. "I will be right back."

The two warriors carry Roger's limp body into the house and find a small bed in the corner and lay him down. It is the first time that they have seen just how badly Roger was beaten. Their blood begin to boil. "Those bastards will pay for this," White Horse growls. "I assure you." White Horse needs to see just how bad Roger is beaten, so Koawa starts to unbutton his shirt.

"Go get your woman," White Horse says, "I got him."

Just when the flood gates open, Koawa has his Sunflower inside and sitting on the floor. He sees her shivering. He grabs the blanket that was on his horse and wraps it around her shoulders.

"Can we start a fire?" she asks

"No Love," he says. "We are too close to the main road. We cannot chance the smoke to be seen."

Sunflower stretches out her leg and flinches.

"Let me see it," Koawa says. He lifts the end of her dress up revealing the beautiful curve of her legs. He examines the wound. "I can see the bullet. It is not too deep."

"Dig it out," she says.

"You sure you want me to do that?" he asks.

"If you don't it, it will get infected."

"Sweetheart this is not going to feel good."

"I don't care. It has to be done," she says

Koawa removes his knife. He looks up at the woman that he treasures more than his own life. "You ready?" he asks. She nods her head yes and he goes in and starts to dig the bullet out. He sees her flinch a little when he starts to dig, but is impressed at how strong she is at handling the pain. He finally is able to get it out.

"Got it," he says. He looks up at her. "You are a true warrior. You know that?"

"I have to be," she smiles. "You can't be the only warrior in this relationship, now can you?"

He smiles over at her. How he is growing deeper and deeper in love with her as the minutes go by. He hears White Horse speak his tongue and comes to his side, as White Horse is tending to Roger's beaten body.

"One of us is going to have to stay awake tonight and keep watch," he says

"Right, I will do it."

"I need to stay with him. I will do it" White Horse says.

"How is he doing?" Koawa asks.

"I am certain he has broken ribs and I am suspicious his arm is too. I wish Medicine Moon was here. I just do not know what to do for him."

"I can find a scout and get word and have her come," Koawa suggests.

"No," White Horse says. "At first light we are leaving. I do not feel safe here. I will make him a travois in the morning. There is no way he can ride. We will stay high in the hills for as long as we can and hope our scouts are able to keep the Blue Coat's away."

"They are not going to stop until they find him and when they do, they will kill him," Koawa says.

"Then I need to make sure they don't find him," White Horse says.

They hear Roger moan. Koawa comes down to him.

"Roger, it's Koawa," he says.

"Corrine," he mumbles.

"She is right here.

"Hurts to breath," he gasps.

Koawa looks up at White Horse. Words do not need to be spoken, as they know each other's thoughts. They both fear that Roger may have injuries that they cannot see. Koawa hears White Horse deeply sigh.

"I will not lose him brother. He saved my life multiple times. I now need to save his."

Although White Horse is clueless on where to begin, as the beating that his brother-in-law has suffered is like none that he has ever seen. He changes the subject by looking across the room at Sunflower.

"You have a good one there," White Horse says.

"I know," Koawa smiles.

"She really pulled through tonight. Most women would not have been so strong."

"I just want her safe," Koawa says.

"She will be, she has you," he smiles.

"I am in love with her White Horse."

"A blind man could see that," he grins. "Go be with her. I am fine here. What Roger needs now is sleep."

Sunflower is curled up against the fireplace wall. Her leg is throbbing. She wraps the blanket further around her chest and leans her head back on the wall and starts to cry. She wipes a tear when she sees Koawa come down by her side.

"How are you doing?" he asks.

"The leg is painful, but I am alright."

Koawa is not fooled. He strokes a curl on the side of her head. He sees her eyes well up. He is quick at putting her in his arms.

"It's alright," he consoles.

"Oh my God I was so scared," she cries.

"I know you were Love."

"I don't know what I am going to do," she cries.

"What do you mean?"

"I cannot go back. I have no money to start over. I don't know where I am going to go."

He takes her hand and places it into his. He then takes his long fingers and cups them over hers.

"This is where you are going," he says.

"I don't understand."

"Your hand and my hand will be together."

"You mean go back home with you?"

"Yes. Let me take care of you. Let me show you my world. I will give you everything. My love, my life, and my home." He kisses her wet cheek. "I love you Sunflower and I want you more than I have ever wanted anything else in my life. I promise you nothing will ever destroy my love for you. If you accept, I promise you a life filled with love and happiness. You will want for nothing."

White Horse is standing by the window looking at the buckets of rain coming down. His mind is heavy in thought. He is grateful for the heavy rain. It will help cover their tracks, as he knows it won't be long until they are picked up again. He thinks of his brother-in-law, who will never be a free man in his world again. He worries he may not make it through the night, as he is certain he has injuries inside that he cannot see. He then thinks of his Prairie Dawn and how hurt she was when he left. He needs to get home to comfort her and mourn their loss of their son together. He remembers their harsh words to each other and the pain that was in her eyes. He has never seen her so angry with him. He only hopes he can make amends, as he loves his wife more than anything.

He looks over at his brother holding the woman that he loves. How gentle he is with her and how obvious his love for her is. He thinks about the soldiers who he has been fighting with for years. How tired he is of all their lies and deception. He knows the fighting will only get worse with his people, even more now due to the escape of their Great Healer. As he turns to look out the window again, he thinks to himself how he wishes he could have done some things differently and turn back the time. He knows he must do everything he can to keep his brother-in-law alive. He must not allow him to die. Whatever it takes he cannot die.

The End

Stay tuned for the 6th book in the Prairie Dawn series, Running Moccasins. Roger becomes a fugitive from the Army which will bring turmoil to the Lakota band who are hiding him. A trade with the Crows will cause havoc. The secrets of a cavern filled with gold will be revealed. A plan will be set into motion that will benefit the future existence of the Lakota band, but will put Koawa's wife in great danger. The marriage of White Horse and Prairie Dawn will be tested. Running Moccasins is an action-packed adventure that will keep you guessing until the end.

Other Books by
Karen Dee Musson

Prairie Dawn

Prairie Dawn Lakota Blues

Prairie Dawn Spirit in the wind

Sioux Pride

About the Author

Karen Dee Musson is the author of the Prairie Dawn series. Karen continues her love and admiration of the Native American culture in her 5th book Native Warrior. Karen lived most of her life in a small town in Northern Illinois and spent twenty-five years in Southern Arizona where her knowledge and respect grew for the Native American culture. Karen currently resides in Northern Texas with her family.

www.ingramcontent.com/pod-product-compliance
Lightning Source LLC
Chambersburg PA
CBHW051640260626
47170CB00004B/1257